EINSTEIN the PENGUIN

THE CASE of the FISHY DETECTIVE

Books by Iona Rangeley

EINSTEIN THE PENGUIN

EINSTEIN THE PENGUIN: THE CASE OF THE FISHY DETECTIVE

EINSTEIN the PENGUIN

THE CASE of the FISHY DETECTIVE

Iona Rangeley

Illustrated by David Tazzyman

HarperCollins *Children's Books*

First published in the United Kingdom by
HarperCollins *Children's Books* in 2022
Published in this edition 2023
HarperCollins *Children's Books* is a division of HarperCollins*Publishers* Ltd
1 London Bridge Street
London SE1 9GF

www.harpercollins.co.uk

HarperCollins*Publishers*,
Macken House, 39/40 Mayor Street Upper,
Dublin 1, D01 C9W8, Ireland

2

ISBN 978-0-00-847603-8

Iona Rangeley and David Tazzyman assert the moral right to be identified as the author and illustrator of the work respectively.

A CIP catalogue record for this title is available from the British Library.

Typeset in Arno Pro Regular 13pt/24pt
Printed and bound in the UK using 100% renewable electricity at CPI Group (UK) Ltd

This book is produced from independently certified FSC™ paper
to ensure responsible forest management.

For more information visit: www.harpercollins.co.uk/green

To Patrick and Molly

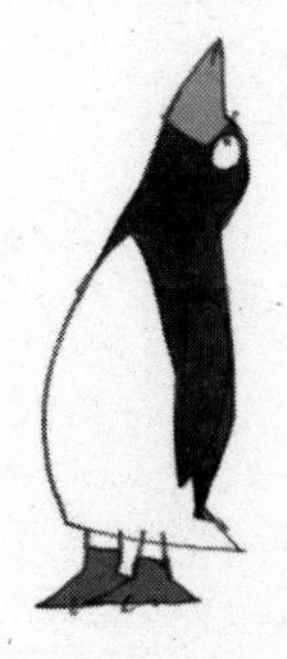

Chapter One

Back to London

Imogen was walking home from school by herself.

Normally she walked with Arthur, but Arthur had gone over to Theo's house, and normally they would get the bus, but today she had missed it – and anyway she was feeling brave.

I must look very grown up, she thought to herself, *walking along a pavement without anyone else.*

And, of course, she *was* very grown up when you thought about it. In three weeks' time she'd be eleven, and that was an impressive sort of age. Ten was double figures too, but not in such a tidy way as eleven. Eleven did double figures properly.

Imogen imagined that once she was eleven she would look and feel quite different. She would be taller and cleverer, and adults would ask her opinion on things and take her responses seriously at last. Walking home alone was simply practice for what was to come.

It was early March, and none of the trees had bothered to grow any leaves yet, so that when the wind blew the branches looked like they were scratching the sky with their claws. But it was warm for March, and Imogen didn't mind the grey: grey was probably a sensible colour, the kind of colour she would appreciate once she was eleven.

She tucked her hands into her pockets and thought about the maths test that she had on Monday, and whether she was going to get an invite to Amy Diggory's birthday party. She didn't like the idea of not being invited, but she didn't much like the idea of going, either. It was all rather confusing to think about. And, while she'd done pretty well in her last maths test, this week Mr Smith had started putting letters into their sums, and Imogen wasn't sure whether she'd understood everything. She didn't see why numbers and letters couldn't be kept separately: when they sat next to each other like that everything went wobbly.

Still – those were problems for next week, thought Imogen, as she opened the garden gate and walked up the path towards her house. And right now it was Friday, which happened to be her favourite day of any day at all.

'It's Friday!' said Imogen, as she burst into the kitchen.

Mrs Stewart was just unpacking her work things, and Mr Stewart – who'd had the day off – was sitting with his feet up in front of the telly.

'So it is,' said Mr Stewart. 'Did they teach you that at school?'

'Can I borrow your laptop to check if the email's here?' Imogen dropped her school bag on to the floor and went to grab a biscuit from the biscuit tin.

'Just one!' said Mrs Stewart. 'And don't you want to wait until Arthur's home? He'll get upset if you open the email without him.'

'Oh,' said Imogen disappointedly. 'But what if it's important? What if Einstein's had some sort of accident, and we won't know about it because we haven't checked?'

'Those emails from Australia are the same every week,' said Mr Stewart. 'Einstein's eaten another fish and been swimming. I'm sure it can wait an hour until your brother's home.'

'It might be different this time,' said Imogen, though she didn't really mind waiting – she just liked having the last word.

'You mean he might have eaten a pilchard rather than an anchovy? Whatever will we do!' said Mr Stewart, and Imogen bounded over to the sofa to thump him with a cushion, then ran upstairs to find a book.

'Still reading about detectives?' said Mrs Stewart when she returned a moment later.

Imogen flopped down on to the sofa and sighed. 'No,' she said. 'Detectives are a bit babyish, I think.'

'Surely not!' said Mrs Stewart, aghast. 'You can't mean that.'

Imogen made a sort of mumbling noise and buried her face in her book. She didn't mean it – not really. She'd loved being a detective, and for months she'd carried her notebook with her at all times, keeping a constant eye out for things that might need investigating. But the truth was that ever since Einstein had left there hadn't been any more mysteries. Or there had – but they weren't the proper kind of mystery, the kind with heroes and villains. There were only boring mysteries: things like how to say 'hello' in French, and why Arthur never wiped his toothpaste up off the basin.

All Imogen had now to remind herself that she'd ever been a detective before were the newspaper clippings Mrs Stewart had insisted on pinning to the fridge:

Imogen Stewart:
The Girl Who Solved
The Penguin Mystery

BRITISH CHILDREN
RETURN MISSING
PENGUIN TO SYDNEY

Penguins Now Most Popular
Animals At Sydney Zoo

They were very good newspaper clippings, to be fair, and Imogen still felt a surge of pride whenever she looked at them. But it had been a whole year now – *more* than a year, in fact. It was only sensible to assume her detective days were behind her.

When Theo's mum dropped Arthur off outside the house, he was so eager to run up the path that he almost forgot to say goodbye. But he stopped himself.

'Thank you for having me!' he blurted. 'And I'll see you on Monday, Theo.'

'Are you in a rush?' Theo's mother asked.

'Oh, no,' said Arthur, going a little pink. 'But Fridays are when Ted emails us. He's the zookeeper from Sydney.'

'Ah, of course,' she said, raising her eyebrows a little. 'Silly me – how could I forget?'

Theo's mum had never actually met Einstein, and she still looked bemused whenever he was mentioned, like she didn't quite believe any of it had really happened.

'Don't worry, Mum. You'll meet Einstein next time he comes to visit,' said Theo.

'Oh, he's coming back, is he?'

'No . . . I don't know,' Arthur admitted. 'I hope so.'

'Well, tell your parents I said hello,' said Theo's mum. She'd become distracted by Theo's little sister, Sophia, who had started crying in the back seat.

Arthur waved one last time before hurrying up the garden path towards the front door.

'Imogen!' cried Arthur, as he crashed into the house and threw his school bag down on top of a pile of old trainers. 'It's Friday!'

'So it is!' called Mr Stewart. 'Did they teach you that at school?'

'That wasn't funny the first time, Dad,' said Imogen. 'Can we use the laptop now? Please?'

'Yes, yes, I demand that you use the laptop!' said

Mr Stewart. 'Why haven't you used it already? This week might be the week that everything changes!'

'You're *still* not *funny*!' said Imogen, but she was already halfway up the stairs.

Dear Imogen and Arthur,

Thank you so much for your email last week! I passed everything you said on to Einstein, and he gave a very big squawk when he heard how well Arthur had done in his maths test.

This week Einstein has done a lot of swimming and has shown a preference for pilchards over anchovies. Here's a picture of him hanging out on a rock with his new friend Steve. They'd just made up after a brief incident this morning when Einstein stole Steve's fish at feeding time. I think he mostly did it because some tourists were watching. Einstein always wants to be in front of a camera . . .!

Best,

Ted

Mr Stewart had been right: it was pretty much the same as normal. But sometimes, Imogen told herself, normal was nice. It was nice knowing that Einstein was safe, and happy, and making friends with other penguins. Nine-year-old Imogen might have felt selfishly about it, and hoped for another adventure, but this Imogen – who was, after all, not so far off eleven – knew that as long as Einstein was safe everything was really all right. She smiled at the photo and started to turn away from the computer.

'Imogen, wait!' said Arthur.

'What?'

'He just sent us another message! He wants to do a video call!'

Imogen spun round. Video calls to Sydney only happened very occasionally.

Just then the desktop started to ring, and Ted's profile picture appeared above the keyboard in front of them.

Imogen rushed to click ACCEPT and the picture expanded to fill the whole screen – only now Ted's face was moving too.

'Hi!' Ted waved, peering into the webcam.

He looked blurry at first, but eventually crackled into real time. He appeared to be in an office – the same one he'd been in last time they had spoken, in fact. Imogen couldn't remember when that was. Three weeks ago? Four?

'Can you hear me?' said Ted.

'What did he say?' whispered Arthur.

'Yes, we can hear you!' said Imogen. 'Can you see us?'

'Our camera's turned off,' said Arthur, and he elbowed Imogen out of the way to change the setting.

'Ah, there you are!' said Ted. 'How's it going?'

'Good,' said Imogen, resting her head awkwardly on her elbow. She always felt oddly shy in video calls, which was unlike her. Seeing her own miniature face in the corner made her self-conscious.

'Well, it's very late here, but I'm on the night shift so I thought I might as well let Einstein say hello.'

Arthur barged his way on to the edge of the desk chair in order to see better. Imogen was hogging it again. 'Where is he?' he asked.

'Shh,' whispered Imogen. 'Ted's *getting* him.'

They watched Ted lean down and scoop something up off the floor, and a few seconds later Einstein appeared, his feet paddling in mid-air as if he hadn't quite noticed where he was yet. Ted placed him down on the desk in front of the computer.

'Look who's here, Einstein!' said Ted.

Einstein glanced up at the screen and squawked excitedly.

'Hi, Einstein!' said Imogen.

He stretched his flippers back into the air and bounced up and down on his little feet.

'We miss you!' said Arthur. 'When are you coming back to London?'

Einstein squawked again and shrugged his flippers, then made several frantic attempts to peck the screen.

'He misses you too,' said Ted. 'Perhaps you kids could visit Sydney sometime.'

'Maybe,' said Imogen uncertainly. 'But we couldn't come alone. Mum and Dad would have to save up for it and take time off work and everything – and we don't know when that would be.'

'Yeah, it's a long way,' Ted agreed.

'We want to, though,' she added.

'You'll still let us know if Einstein ever comes to England, won't you?' asked Arthur.

'Arthur, there's no one else I would dream of telling first.'

Arthur smiled and sat back in the chair. He liked Ted. Ted always said the right thing.

'Well, I'm afraid I'm going to have to pack up in a minute, but let's talk again soon.' Ted ruffled Einstein's feathers and handed him a snack.

'Okay. See you soon, Einstein,' said Imogen. She brushed her finger against the screen, as if she was stroking Einstein's feathers too.

'Bye, Einstein!' said Arthur.

Einstein squawked so enthusiastically that he dropped the snack he was eating, then hurried to pick it up again and tripped over the keyboard. The picture turned the colour of feathers as Einstein came crashing towards the screen.

Imogen and Arthur heard him squawk once more before he pushed himself up with his flippers and accidentally ended the call with the edge of his beak.

Chapter Two

Return to the Zoo

Arthur stared down at the surface of the table and traced his fingers along the woodgrain. It wasn't a very interesting table, but he wasn't in the mood to stare at anything else.

He wondered about going to find Imogen, but she was upstairs, reading her book, and Mr Stewart was out at work. The house felt boring and quiet. Arthur thought crossly that there was no point in a weekend that was so boring and quiet: he might as well go to school and sit by himself in the playground for all the fun he was having.

Across the kitchen, Mrs Stewart was talking loudly in her telephone voice.

'Yes, yes. Now, I'm afraid, I *do* have to go . . .'

Arthur glanced up at her, then over at the photos on the fridge – photos of Einstein, photos of everyone – then gave up and went on staring at the table.

'What's the matter?' said Mrs Stewart a few moments later. She had put the phone down now and pulled a chair out to sit at the table beside him.

'Nothing,' said Arthur glumly.

'You look sad.'

Arthur thought about this. 'We spoke to Einstein yesterday,' he said.

He wasn't sure at what point his happiness had turned to sadness. He supposed it must have happened overnight.

'Ah,' said Mrs Stewart knowingly. 'I see.' She thought for a moment, and the clock ticked loudly on the wall. 'Well, how about we go to the zoo again?'

Arthur looked surprised.

'We could go to see the penguins. It might be fun. They'll remind you of him!'

Arthur frowned. He supposed it did sound better than sitting around at home. He'd always liked going to the zoo, hadn't he? Even before Einstein, it had been one of his favourite places in London.

'Okay,' he agreed after a moment.

By the time they reached the penguin enclosure at London Zoo that afternoon, Arthur was almost in a good mood. He'd cheered up enough to nag Mrs Stewart for an ice cream – it wasn't really the weather for ice cream, but that never seemed to matter on a day out – and he rushed ahead to get as close as he could to the glass wall. Mrs Stewart and Imogen followed closely behind him.

For several minutes, Arthur watched the penguins

dipping in and out of the water, and waddling about on the rocks. He liked imagining what all their names were, and which penguin was friends with which. One of them even approached him for a moment, and seemed to stare him directly in the eye.

Arthur was just about to shout for Imogen to come and look when it abruptly waddled off again, distracted by another visitor. For some reason, Arthur's heart sank.

Imogen didn't seem to care about the penguins. She had watched them with him for a while, and then all of a sudden she'd disappeared to sit on the steps with Mrs Stewart. She'd even taken her book out of her rucksack. Arthur scowled in her general direction, then turned back to the enclosure.

'Hi, I'm Arthur,' he found himself saying out loud to a penguin that was waddling by.

A boy standing next to him sniggered.

Arthur felt his chest tighten in embarrassment. He supposed that the boy was right to snigger: the penguin hardly even glanced at him. It just went on waddling, as if there was nothing to say and nothing was the matter.

Arthur wandered back to the steps. He sat down, put his elbows on his knees and rested his chin in his hands.

Many, many miles away, across the world and upside down, a different penguin *was* looking through the walls of its enclosure.

Einstein appeared to have noticed the brother and sister from a long way off. The girl was holding a notebook, and the boy was clinging nervously to his mother's arm.

Einstein had spent the whole morning eating fish – rather more than his fair share, in fact – and was feeling far too full to move. For that reason, staring at the approaching family suited him very well.

Out of the corner of his eye he noticed a pigeon fluttering down to land in a nearby tree and turned round to squawk at it. The pigeon cocked its head and blinked at him, and Einstein narrowed his eyes.

They stared at each other for a few more seconds, and then Einstein squawked once more – a loud, bossy squawk that came from the bottom of his chest.

This time the pigeon got the message and, shooting Einstein a dirty look, flew off to land on a tree above the crocodile pen.

What had he been thinking about before? That was right – the family!

Einstein glanced around desperately. He couldn't see them any more. A small boy was trying to catch his attention from the other side of the glass, but his hair was the wrong colour. None of the children who visited him nowadays were ever *quite right.*

'Mummy, look at that penguin!'

The brother and sister he had been watching before reappeared out of the crowd, and Einstein craned forward to look at them. It couldn't be . . . surely . . . was it?

'Lily, look – he's staring at us!'

The girl glanced down at Einstein. 'Aw, he's cute,' she said. 'But the monkeys are still my favourite.'

It wasn't them. The girl was too tall to be Imogen, and the boy was wearing a football shirt, which Arthur would never have done. Arthur was rubbish at sports. And, besides, their accents were different – more like Ted's.

Just then a zookeeper arrived with a bucket of pilchards, and Einstein rushed away to crash belly-first into the water, swiftly forgetting what had attracted his attention in the first place.

Up on the steps, Imogen slammed her book shut and sighed. It was all very well reading grown-up books, but apart from *seeming* grown-up she couldn't see the point of them.

This one didn't even have pictures. Not needing pictures was very clever and everything, but it wasn't much fun. And anyway the story was no good. There were no mysteries and no evil villains. Just a girl who went on about horses.

All of a sudden, Imogen decided that she couldn't stand horses. They were too tall and had too many legs.

She spotted Arthur sitting a few steps below her and went down to join him. 'Mum says we have to go in a minute.'

Arthur jumped. He had almost forgotten where he was. He stared round at the penguins, then up at his sister.

'Are you okay?' Imogen asked.

'None of them are Einstein,' said Arthur.

Imogen looked confused. 'That's because Einstein's in Sydney.'

'I know,' said Arthur, 'but I was thinking . . .'

He wasn't entirely sure what he'd been thinking: he wasn't good at planning things out from start to finish, like Imogen was. Only he knew that the things he'd been thinking were important.

'I was wondering if we should ask Ted if Einstein can come back. I really miss him.'

Imogen looked at him and put on her big-sister voice. 'We've asked him before, Arthur. Ted can't just send him over. He doesn't own the zoo. It's not that simple.'

'I know!' protested Arthur. 'I'm not saying we do anything simple. We can do something complicated!'

'Like what?'

'I don't know,' Arthur admitted. 'But we agreed before Einstein left. Dad said that we could try, and you – *you* said it was only goodbye till we saw him again!'

'Did I?' said Imogen. She liked that idea: it sounded like a very clever thing to have said.

'And you can't say that and then just never want to see him at all!' said Arthur crossly.

'I do want to see him,' said Imogen. 'I just – it's not that simple . . .'

As a matter of fact, she had tried her best not to think about it. She'd always imagined that Einstein would come back to them at some point; but, if Imogen thought about it properly, she would have to entertain the possibility that he might never return to London. And frankly it was much easier to focus on nice things, like the fact that Einstein was safe and happy and had a new friend called Steve.

'I don't think we should give up just because it isn't *simple*,' said Arthur.

Imogen nodded. 'Yeah,' she said slowly. 'You're right.'

'So can we email Ted and ask?'

Imogen paused. 'Not yet,' she said after a moment. 'If we're going to do something, we have to do something clever.'

Chapter Three

A Plan Begins

'What's that in your pocket, Imogen?' said Mrs Stewart loudly.

Imogen scowled. 'Nothing.'

They were walking over to their grandparents' house for Sunday lunch, and the warm weather – in a fit of frustration before it turned into spring – had disappeared suddenly amid the drizzle.

'It's your detective notebook!' Mrs Stewart went on. 'It *is*! I haven't seen that thing in forever!'

Imogen's cheeks felt hot. She thought about darting

away, but the road was busy, and anyway they were sharing an umbrella.

'James, Imogen's got her detective notebook!' Mrs Stewart called over her shoulder to her husband. 'What's going on then? Do we have another mystery?'

'Stop it, Mum!' Imogen blurted. 'Mind your own business!'

'Imogen Stewart! Do not speak to me like that!'

'Sorry,' said Imogen quickly. She hadn't really meant it, but her mum was always poking her nose into things at the wrong time.

'You do not tell me to mind my own business. I'm your mother!'

'Sorry,' said Imogen again.

They walked the length of the final street in silence, Mrs Stewart sniffing occasionally to remind everyone that she was cross. The pavements smelled the way pavements do when they get wet after having spent a long time being dry, and Imogen kept her eyes on the ground, to avoid stepping on any of the cracks.

Grandpa Stewart had made roast beef for lunch. It was a bit dry, thought Imogen: usually Grandma did the cooking, but she had started doing funny things lately, like forgetting what day it was and leaving her keys in the oven, so the job had fallen to Grandpa.

'The thing about beef,' Grandpa was solemnly explaining to Arthur, 'is to roast it for a very, very long time.'

Mr and Mrs Stewart appeared to be giggling at each other, but

Imogen had missed the joke. She stirred a roast potato round in her gravy and thought about Einstein. She'd been thinking about him all weekend. Arthur was expecting her to come up with something – she knew he was – but it didn't always feel like there was anything left to come up with. Einstein was in Sydney, and they were in London. Going to Australia was expensive, and Einstein belonged to a zoo. What could Imogen possibly do about any of that?

'How's school, Imogen?' said Grandma.

Imogen almost jumped. Grandma had been so quiet throughout the meal.

'Good, thanks,' she said.

'And what are you thinking about?'

Grandma always asked that question. Back when she was little, Imogen had found it annoying: she wasn't always thinking anything, and, even when she was thinking about something, it didn't mean she wanted everyone to know about it. If she'd wanted that, she would have just opened her mouth and talked. But Grandma looked expectant, and all of a sudden Imogen didn't want to disappoint her.

'I'm thinking about our penguin,' said Imogen. 'We haven't seen him for over a year.'

'Well, why don't you visit him?' Grandma suggested.

'We can't,' Imogen explained. 'He lives in Sydney. In a zoo.'

'Ah, zoos!' said Grandma, and she gave a knowing nod. 'I used to go to the zoo.'

'Really?'

'Yes, yes,' said Grandma. 'I always felt a bit sorry for the animals, but I did love the shows they put on. They brought animals in from all over the world, you know!'

Imogen frowned. 'From all over the world?' she repeated.

Grandma took a sip of her water and then seemed to forget what she was talking about. 'What's that about the world, dear?'

'You said the zoo used to have shows with animals from all over the world?'

'It did?' said Grandma. 'Isn't that nice. Do you like the zoo?'

'No, I'm not sure I do,' said Imogen quietly.

'Right, who wants pudding?' asked Grandpa, slapping his hands together and heading into the kitchen.

Normally she was the first to want pudding, but Imogen's mind was racing. She hadn't even finished her potatoes. Of course, no zoo would send a penguin halfway round the world just for a catch-up with some old friends; but there were *some* things they would send a penguin halfway round the world for, weren't there? After all, that's what they'd done with Isaac, Einstein's friend who had been transferred from Sydney to Edinburgh. If only Imogen could come up with something – something important enough to justify it . . .

Arthur could tell that his sister was thinking because she had tucked her hair behind her ears and hardly touched her custard, which was starting to form cold lumps at the edge of her bowl.

'What is it?' he hissed. Their parents had finished their pudding and followed Grandpa outside to look at a problem with his car tyre, and Grandma had gone upstairs for her afternoon nap. 'Have you had an idea?'

Imogen shook her head. 'It has to be something worth the zoo's time . . .' she said, thinking aloud.

'What does?'

'If we want Einstein to come to London, we need a better excuse than just missing him.'

'They let him stay with us the Christmas before last when they didn't have to,' Arthur pointed out. 'Maybe they'll do it again if we just ask nicely enough.'

'Maybe, but then why hasn't he been allowed to visit already? Granny mentioned something about animal shows . . .'

'A show?' said Arthur. 'What, like a circus?'

Imogen shrugged.

'But Einstein can't do any tricks,' said Arthur. 'And he might not enjoy it.'

'That's true,' Imogen admitted. 'I wouldn't want him to have to do something he wouldn't enjoy.'

Arthur paused. 'You don't think they ever found out about what we did to that detective, do you?'

Imogen's stomach gave a squirm. She hadn't thought about Detective Bill Hunter in forever – not since they had tied him up with masking tape and covered his head with a mop bucket. Something which, she hurriedly reminded herself, he'd thoroughly deserved, trying to keep Einstein from reuniting with Isaac like that.

'I just wondered,' Arthur went on. 'I had a nightmare about him the other night. You don't think *he's* stopping Einstein from coming back, do you?'

'What do you mean?' said Imogen.

'Well, wasn't he working for Sydney Zoo?'

'Ted said the reason Einstein couldn't come back was just an administration thing,' said Imogen, although, come to think of it, she couldn't remember what administration meant, and now Arthur had made her worry. 'But maybe we should google him.'

Their parents were still busy outside, and Grandpa's computer was sitting temptingly in the corner, its screensaver flickering at them.

'Just quickly,' she added. 'Before Mum and Dad come back.'

Arthur glanced at the window, then ran over to the computer. 'Detective Will Hunter,' he dictated to himself as he typed.

'*Bill*,' Imogen corrected him. 'It was Detective *Bill* Hunter.'

'Inactive,' said Arthur, puzzled.

A webpage had appeared with Bill Hunter's face in the top right-hand corner. This private detective is no longer operating, it read. Several one- and two-star reviews were visible towards the bottom.

'What?' said Imogen, peering over Arthur's shoulder. 'So he just isn't working any more?'

'No,' said Arthur. 'Maybe he decided he wanted to do something else.'

'Maybe,' agreed Imogen, although that didn't sound very *like* him, from the little she knew. 'But at least we know he's not interfering with anything. So there – you don't need to worry.'

Arthur clicked the back button on the webpage.

'Hang on,' said Imogen. 'What's that?'

There was another result underneath the first – a video. Arthur clicked on it, and a voice blared out from the computer at full volume.

'And today we're speaking to Bill Hunter. Bill, what brought you into the advertising industry?'

Arthur hurriedly turned the volume down. Detective Bill Hunter's pale, sinister face appeared on the screen, and he smiled leeringly at the man interviewing him.

'Yes, well, I used to be a private detective, you see, but I had to give it up after I was viciously attacked by a – well, I shouldn't say his name, really,

because he's been in the public eye himself. But my time away from work prompted a lot of reflection on where my career was going, and that was when I realised that my true passion in life was to be an agent representing animal actors in advertising.'

'Relatable for many of our viewers, I'm sure. And, of course, it was you who cast this advert for carpets, wasn't it?'

The two men went on chattering, and Imogen and Arthur stared at each other.

'Viciously attacked?' Arthur repeated.

'It seems like a *bit* of an exaggeration, doesn't it?' said Imogen.

'He had to take time off work!' said Arthur.

'Well, he shouldn't have tried to stop us from finding Isaac!'

'He was only doing his job!'

'Who was only doing his job?' Mr Stewart's voice sounded from the doorway.

Imogen and Arthur froze, so much so that it took several seconds before Arthur recovered his senses enough to press **PAUSE**. In the background Bill Hunter's voice was chatting away about moving to a studio in London.

'No one,' said Imogen. 'We were just talking about a movie.'

Mr Stewart narrowed his eyes. 'That's not what it sounded like to me.'

Imogen said nothing. She had a feeling Mr Stewart might have been at the door for rather longer than they realised.

'You were talking about Einstein,' said Mr Stewart, and he came into the room and closed the door behind him. 'And you're not leaving until you tell me why.'

CHAPTER FOUR

An Apology

'Is that it?' asked Arthur.

The building looked big and scary, standing several floors above the street and squinting down at them from its tiny concrete windows.

'That's the address,' said Mr Stewart, and he turned round in the driver's seat to eye them both suspiciously. He had driven them straight over from school. 'I'll be waiting right here in the car. Off you go and apologise.'

Imogen had thought about how to word the

letter all week. She still wasn't sure she had forgiven Detective Bill Hunter – nor did she particularly regret anything, except perhaps getting caught. After all, if he'd had it his way, Einstein would have gone straight back to Sydney without seeing Isaac or getting any Christmas presents. Besides, the mission had been important, and she'd only been little then. But she

somewhat reluctantly supposed that Mr Stewart was right when he told her apologising was the grown-up thing to do. She was nearly eleven now, after all.

Eventually she'd decided that simple was best:

Dear Mr Bill Hunter,

We just wanted to say we are very sorry for attacking you with a penguin and tying you up and all that stuff. It was a long time ago, but we didn't mean it in a bad way and it definitely won't happen again.

From Imogen and Arthur Stewart

The letter was in her pocket, folded up in one of Mrs Stewart's prettiest envelopes – the ones she kept for thank-you cards. Imogen had even stuffed some chocolate buttons inside for good measure.

She pursed her lips and sank a little further down in her seat.

'You're going to have to get out of the car eventually,' Mr Stewart pointed out. 'You're just lucky I haven't told your mother.'

Arthur followed as Imogen slowly climbed out on to the pavement.

'Do we go in?' asked Arthur.

'Yes,' said Imogen, but neither of them moved.

'When?' said Arthur after a moment.

Imogen took a deep breath and marched towards the revolving door. It was made of glass, and it glinted as it swung them into a small reception room with a wooden floor and potted plants dotted here and there beside the windows. An oldish woman was tapping away at a keyboard behind the tall white desk. Just as they entered the room, she ducked through another door into what looked like a room full of files.

Imogen waited a moment for the woman to return.

'Hello?' she said when the moment had passed.

A pair of catlike reading glasses had been abandoned on the desk, strange ones with jewelled edges and a chain dangling down on either side. Imogen almost found herself reaching out to fiddle with them, but resisted.

'Can I help you?' called a bored-sounding voice eventually.

'*Imogen*,' Arthur hissed. 'Say something!'

He wasn't good at talking to strangers, and tended to pass messages via his family, like a sort of whispering game.

'Yes,' said Imogen, frowning, and was about to launch into the little speech she had prepared when it occurred to her that perhaps, if she got on with it, they could avoid having to speak to anyone at all.

'We have a letter for somebody who works here!' she announced. She pulled the envelope from her pocket and slapped it down on to the desk. 'We'll just leave it here if that's all right?'

'Thank you for your help!' said Arthur, and they spun round and rushed towards the door.

Imogen relaxed her shoulders as they made it out

on to the pavement. She even let go of Arthur's hand. It had been hot inside the reception room, and the breeze rustling down the street felt like its own little breath of relief.

'Imogen,' said Arthur nervously.

'It's okay. We've done it now. We don't have to think about him ever again.'

'Imogen, he's following us . . .'

Detective Bill Hunter had appeared out of the revolving doors and was striding towards them along the street, his long white coat billowing out behind him.

Imogen whipped round, and her eyes widened.

'Hey, kids!' he cried.

'Leave us alone!' shouted Arthur. He wanted to run away, but his feet felt rooted to the ground.

'Don't annoy him,' hissed Imogen. 'Let's just be polite and then get away as quickly as we can.' She turned to face Detective Bill Hunter. 'Hello,' she said quietly.

'I'm glad you found me so quickly,' he said, as he

caught up with them. 'Thank you for the chocolate buttons.'

'Oh, thank you,' said Imogen vaguely.

She wasn't sure why she was thanking him for thanking her, and suddenly the idea of a chocolate-button-based apology seemed absurd.

'I just wanted to say no hard feelings, all right?'

'Huh?' said Imogen.

'I'm accepting your apology,' he said. 'It's fine. I was never made to be a detective. You beat me at my own game. I take my hat off to you.'

Arthur glanced up at Bill Hunter's head. It was true: he wasn't wearing a hat.

'Oh,' said Imogen. 'Well, good. We'll be off then.'

'Hang on. Why don't you come into the office for a cup of coffee?'

'We have to go home,' said Imogen, glancing sideways at her father's car, which was still a little way up the street.

'And we don't drink coffee,' Arthur added. 'Coffee's for grown-ups.'

'A hot chocolate then,' Bill suggested. 'Just a quick one. Five minutes. To put any bad feelings behind us.'

Imogen checked her watch.

'My assistant makes the best hot chocolate in London,' he went on.

'All right,' said Imogen slowly.

She didn't see that it could do much harm – and, besides, if they were rude to him now, wouldn't that stop their apology from counting? Mr Stewart would probably send them straight back in to apologise all over again, and that would be even worse.

'But we really can't stay longer than five minutes.'

Bill Hunter led them back inside and up in a cramped elevator, then down two empty, echoing corridors. Arthur glanced into a few of the rooms they passed, but they all appeared abandoned. It was funny: the building looked so grand from outside, but inside it seemed to be falling apart.

Bill's office, however, was far from empty. A big black fan whirred on the ceiling above their heads, and the whole room felt oddly cold. Several spiky cacti lined the window ledge, and the walls were pasted with notes and pieces of paper – they looked like they might have been storyboards.

'Well, this is my life now!' said Bill Hunter proudly, as he flopped back into his leather swivel chair and planted his hands on top of his slightly rounded stomach.

Imogen and Arthur sat down at the table in the centre of the room. Arthur shivered.

'Get this boy his hot chocolate!' called Bill Hunter, slapping the table and making Arthur jump. 'Can't you see that he's cold?' Then he sat back and laughed, as if he hadn't really meant it.

A few minutes later, a woman came bustling through the door with a loaded tray. 'Cream and marshmallows?' she asked, in an uninterested voice, without really looking at either of them.

'Ooh, yes please!' said Imogen, and Arthur nodded enthusiastically.

She took a canister of whipped cream from the tray and gave each of them a healthy dollop before setting the mugs of hot chocolate in front of them. Then she handed Bill Hunter a cup of coffee, dolloped some whipped cream on top of that too, and retreated silently out of the door.

'So are you very important now?' asked Arthur curiously.

Bill Hunter chuckled in delight. 'I suppose I am,' he said, and he held his hands out in a sort of helpless shrug.

'You must have become important very quickly,' Imogen pointed out. 'Seeing as you only left your detective work a year ago.'

He smiled tightly. 'What can I say? As I told you, being a detective wasn't my destiny like it is yours. *You* helped me realise that, Imogen.'

'I did?' said Imogen. She liked the idea: that being a detective was really her destiny. Perhaps Detective Bill Hunter wasn't so terrible, after all.

'I'm much happier now,' he went on. 'I arrange for animals to appear in adverts. Perhaps you've seen my latest one, for the carpet shop? With the cat?'

Imogen and Arthur glanced up at the wall above Bill Hunter's head, which was covered in framed stills from the advert, as well as a large and slightly out-of-focus picture of his smiling face. They both shook their heads and looked blank.

'No? It's very famous. But never mind! It's healthy for kids your age not to waste their lives in front of the telly,' he said cheerily, although Arthur could have sworn that for a moment – just a moment – he had looked cross.

'We do watch telly,' said Imogen. 'We just haven't seen that advert. What carpet shop was it for?'

Arthur nudged her. He had a feeling that she ought to be quiet.

'You wouldn't have heard of it,' said Bill Hunter vaguely. 'It's closed. Now, how are those penguin friends of yours? I've wanted to ask for *so* long. You know, it's funny – I've been thinking of reaching out to you myself.'

'You have?' said Arthur.

'Einstein's in Sydney,' Imogen said with a sigh. 'We want him to visit, but we can't think of a good enough excuse. I don't think the zoo will let him travel for no reason. They probably think it's too dangerous.'

'And Isaac's still in Edinburgh,' added Arthur.

Just then the phone rang, and Bill Hunter put his finger in the air, asking for silence.

'Hello?' he said. 'Yes. Yes. We've got plenty of animals. What do you need?' He curled the phone cord between his wiry fingers. 'Let's see . . . We've got, erm, fluffy cats. And tabby cats. Did I mention fluffy cats? All right, fine. Call me back.'

He put the phone down and placed the palm of his hand over his heart. 'What a conundrum!' he said earnestly. 'So you haven't seen your beloved Einstein for over a year?'

Arthur shook his head and took a big sip of his hot chocolate. Bill Hunter had been right: it was one of the best hot chocolates he'd ever tasted. The marshmallows seemed to melt on impact as they touched his tongue.

'Yes,' said Bill Hunter, seeing the look of satisfaction

on Arthur's face. 'I used to love those hot chocolates when I was your age.'

Arthur looked confused. 'You've had the same assistant since you were my age?'

'Don't be stupid, Arthur,' said Imogen, determined to bring the conversation back to Einstein. 'But yes, it's been more than a year.'

'If only there were some way I could help,' said Bill Hunter. He drummed his fingers on the table, then frowned and looked up at the wall, as if something was occurring to him. 'Perhaps there *is* a way . . .'

Imogen and Arthur looked at each other.

'What do you mean?' Imogen prompted.

'It just so happens that I'm looking for some animals to star in a fishfinger advert,' he said. 'How would Einstein and Isaac like to share the role?'

They gaped at him.

'It would be shot right here in my studio. So, of course, for as long as the filming went on, you could spend as much time with your friends as you like. Perhaps we could even arrange for Einstein to stay at your house?'

'Are you sure?' said Imogen in amazement.

It was the perfect solution – and, unlike a performance at a zoo, which had been her only idea so far, Einstein might actually enjoy himself. He loved being in front of the camera, didn't he? That was why he'd had so many Polaroid photos of himself the first time he visited.

'Well, I'd have to contact both zoos, of course, and it's really down to them to grant permission. But I'm more than happy to do the paperwork, and we pay very well – so these sorts of places *tend* to agree to our terms.'

'That would be amazing!' said Imogen.

'Please!' said Arthur. 'Please, please, please!'

Bill Hunter held his hands up in the air. 'But you know,' he breezed, 'that I can't make any promises.'

'You can't?' Arthur sounded crestfallen.

'Not *absolute* ones,' he said. 'But I'm a man of my word. And I can give you my word that I'll try. And between you and me, Arthur, I've pulled this kind of thing off before.' He winked.

Chapter Five

Einstein Returns

For the next week, Imogen couldn't concentrate on anything at all. She sat in French and thought about Einstein. She sat with her friends at lunch and thought about Einstein. Once she even found herself answering 'penguin' when Mr Smith asked her what 3a minus 2a was, and the rest of the class erupted in stifled giggles as she corrected herself.

Arthur was a little less sure of things. He wanted to see Einstein as much as ever, he wanted to see him at least as much as Imogen did, but hadn't it all been too easy? And until Bill Hunter had suggested the idea, turning everything into a whirlwind of overexcitement, he hadn't struck Arthur as particularly trustworthy. Perhaps it was the way he laughed, or the way he smiled while looking cross, or the way he had terrifyingly threatened their friend the year before, but there was something about him that didn't add up. Something Arthur couldn't put his finger on.

Still, he hadn't felt brave enough to dampen everyone's spirits. Even his parents, who had been so sensible about sending Einstein home a year ago, had been far too excited about the prospect of his return to get very cross about Imogen and Arthur's kerfuffle with the detective.

Mrs Stewart had done her best to seem disappointed, but it hadn't been very convincing. After Mr Stewart had explained everything, she had stalked round the kitchen for ten minutes, saying she couldn't *believe* they had got into a fight with a detective without telling her, that she hadn't brought them up to act that way, that they should never keep secrets from their parents again.

But then Arthur had caught her fishing Einstein's blankets out of the airing cupboard and ironing them, even though they were already ironed; and later that day he noticed that Mr Stewart had added herrings to their supermarket order, and wouldn't stop whistling, and Arthur decided that everything was okay – he was probably just worrying about silly things again.

But at the weekend, just before they were due to drive to the airport, he decided to share his concerns with Imogen.

'Why do you have to be such a scaredy-cat, Arthur?' said Imogen irritably. 'You're scared of *everything*!'

'But we don't know Bill – not properly!'

'We didn't know Einstein before he came to stay

with us! Why don't *you* come up with a better plan if you're such an expert?'

'I just don't want anything to go wrong,' said Arthur quietly. He didn't like it when Imogen got cross with him. She could be very scary sometimes.

'Well, maybe you should have said that a week ago – not right before Einstein is about to arrive!'

Imogen already felt bad for snapping at her brother, but of course she didn't like Bill Hunter much, either. He was all right, but she didn't actively *like* him. She couldn't magically start liking someone she had always been afraid of. But they didn't have much of a choice, did they? It was their only plan for getting Einstein back to London – and, if it meant having to put up with the odd hot chocolate in the company of Bill Hunter, then wasn't it worth it?

Besides, Arthur would only have asked her to think up a new plan if they'd decided against it. She wouldn't have minded his complaining if he came up with any ideas as well, but all he did was worry!

She flounced up the stairs to read her book.

Imogen and Arthur soon forgot their fight.

Arthur ignored her for an hour or so in the afternoon, and during that hour he decided that she was probably right – that nothing was going to go wrong, and there wasn't anything to be afraid of. Then, on the way to the airport, once excitement had fully replaced any nerves, they became friends again. They were just starting to talk to each other when the electronic voice on the sat nav pronounced the word 'terminal' in a strange way, and something about it was so funny that they couldn't stop giggling for the rest of the drive.

Mrs Stewart complained that she wasn't able to hear the directions any more, but Arthur couldn't help it. Einstein was coming home, and everything was funny. He had just about managed to stop laughing once Mrs

Stewart was navigating the turnings into the airport car park, but then Imogen leaned over and whispered 'terminal' in his ear, and he started up again.

They were still laughing when they climbed out of the car and began to approach the terminal building.

'Termin-Al,' said Imogen, like a robot, and Arthur doubled over in hysterics.

'All right, you two,' said Mr Stewart. 'We're trying to reassure Mr Hunter that you're not a pair of lunatics, so best behaviour now.'

'Mr Hunter,' Arthur repeated quietly.

Imogen shrugged at him. She agreed that it sounded strange.

Mr and Mrs Stewart had arranged everything with Bill Hunter over the phone. Einstein was arriving from Australia by plane. Both Bill Hunter and the Stewarts would meet him at the airport, and then the Stewarts would take him home, ready to drop him off at Bill Hunter's studio on Monday – the same day Isaac was due to arrive from Edinburgh by train. Until then they had the whole weekend together, and what was even more exciting was that, *after* Monday, both Einstein and Isaac would be spending their evenings with the Stewarts.

'Won't it be fun!' said Mrs Stewart. 'We're like a hotel for film stars! We should put a red carpet up the stairs.'

'But you never let Einstein *go* upstairs,' Arthur pointed out.

'And the carpet's already red,' Imogen added.

'Not after everything you've spilled on it,' said Mr Stewart. 'Look, do you think that's him over there?'

Arthur gasped. It was Einstein! Of course it was Einstein. He was straight ahead of them, appearing out of the sliding doors, his flipper in the hand of the flight attendant who had been escorting him. Arthur could tell it was Einstein straight away, even when he had to squint through the blinding sun. Nobody else waddled like that – and, as it happened, nobody else was a penguin.

'Einstein!' he cried and started to run.

Imogen raced after him. They dodged several luggage trolleys, and almost lost sight of him as they navigated the zebra crossing, but before long Arthur had caught up with him and scooped him up into a great big hug. Imogen appeared a second later, and put her arms round them both.

They stood like that for a long moment, Einstein squawking ecstatically and nibbling at their clothes.

Eventually he squawked to be put back down on the floor, where he bounced about, shaking his tail and flapping his flippers. Imogen crouched down to scratch his tummy, just the way he liked it, and Einstein squawked again and tried to nibble her hand.

Mr and Mrs Stewart had appeared behind them now, and Mrs Stewart was already kneeling down to tidy Einstein's feathers. 'You'll need a bath after a long flight like that,' she said.

Einstein looked blank, and she patted him on the head.

'Hello,' she said to the flight attendant, standing up again, and then the grown-ups started talking about something. Imogen and Arthur were much too excited to concern themselves with what, and continued to fuss over Einstein until he got distracted by a cat being whisked into a nearby taxi and tried to follow it.

'No, Einstein!' said Imogen. 'Don't disappear when you've only just got here.'

'He probably thinks it's our cat,' Arthur pointed out. 'Don't worry, Einstein. Gizmo's at home.'

'That would be a shame, wouldn't it?' came a voice.

Imogen and Arthur jumped and turned round.

Bill Hunter had appeared behind them, smiling his sickliest smile. He was still in his white coat – did he ever wear anything else? Imogen wondered.

Instinctively, she scooped Einstein up off the floor and held him close, tucked under her arm. She'd known Bill Hunter was coming, of course, but something about the action was automatic.

'What would?' asked Arthur. 'Our cat being at home?'

Bill Hunter smiled and stepped closer to stroke Einstein's feathers.

'Why would that be a shame?' Arthur went on. 'Our cat's always at home. He doesn't even really like leaving the house.'

Bill Hunter looked slightly annoyed. 'I *meant—*' he began, but before he got a chance to explain what he meant Einstein had bitten him on the hand.

'Argh!' cried Bill Hunter, his face turning pink with anger. He looked ready to hit someone.

'Ah! Bill, is it?' said Mr Stewart, and he strode over to shake Bill Hunter by his wounded hand.

He unfurled it reluctantly – Imogen didn't think she could see a mark on it at all – and accepted Mr Stewart's introduction as the pink in his face turned gradually back to white.

'Yes, yes, that's me.' He tittered. 'We'll have to fix that penguin's nasty biting habit if he's going to get along on set.'

'Biting?' said Mr Stewart. 'Einstein! What's got into you?'

'There must be some mistake,' Mrs Stewart insisted. 'Einstein doesn't bite.'

'He might have assumed that your hand was a fish,' said Mr Stewart helpfully.

Bill Hunter smiled. 'Yes, you're right. That must have been it. I understand completely.'

Arthur stared up at him warily, but as the conversation between the adults continued his stomach slowly unknotted itself. Most people would look cross after being bitten, after all. Even Mr Stewart might have looked angry in that situation. Einstein just didn't understand that Bill Hunter was their friend now. Well, maybe not their *friend,* but certainly not their enemy.

'So lovely to meet you both properly,' Bill Hunter was saying, and Mr Stewart mumbled something about popping over for a cup of tea next week.

Chapter Six

The National Gallery

'No, get him to catch the fishfinger in his beak!' shouted Arthur.

Imogen took another fishfinger off the plate beside her and threw it into the air for Einstein to catch. Gizmo, who was perched on the edge of the sofa, reached out and clawed at it, but Einstein came away victorious, collapsing on to the carpet in a smattering of crumbs.

Imogen cheered. She could almost see where Bill Hunter was coming from: making adverts was fun –

more fun than being a detective, perhaps. They had been 'practising' Einstein's advert all morning, using the leftovers from the feast Mr and Mrs Stewart had prepared for his return the night before.

The feast had been impressive. Einstein had eaten sardines and herrings and pilchards, and then, when you'd have almost thought he was too full to move, he gobbled down the anchovy ice cream that Mr Stewart had invented earlier that afternoon. Even Arthur, who at only seven already had a knack for eating, was impressed.

'What are you two doing?' asked Mr Stewart suspiciously.

'We're helping Einstein be a film star,' said Imogen, throwing another fishfinger in the air.

This time Einstein missed it – he had become distracted by the cartoon Arthur was half-heartedly drawing on the back of his homework – and the fishfinger bounced off the back of his head and back up towards the sofa, where Gizmo caught it between his paws. Even Gizmo looked surprised at his own coordination. He was just digging into the snack when Einstein – focused again – leaped at him and tore the fishfinger in half. Gizmo hissed, the hair on his back standing on end, while Einstein gave a triumphant little squawk and waddle-ran to hide behind an armchair.

Mr Stewart scooped Gizmo up before he could get any angrier.

'Perhaps we all need to get out of the house,' he said. 'I have a feeling we might destroy it otherwise.'

Gizmo chose that moment to leap, screeching, from Mr Stewart's arms, and took down a lampshade with the edge of his tail.

'Can Einstein come?' asked Arthur.

'Well, we're not leaving him here with that cat.'

Eventually Mr Stewart decided that he would take everyone to the National Gallery. Mr Stewart liked

museums and art galleries, and he liked dragging Imogen and Arthur along with him, especially on Sundays. They didn't *mind* it exactly, although Imogen's feet sometimes hurt, and Arthur would get bothered by the crowds. Today, though, they'd

have been happy going anywhere at all.

For some reason best known to the sky, it had started to drizzle, and little raindrops were popping lightly against the dry pavements and the top of Mr Stewart's black umbrella.

Einstein ducked quietly into Arthur's backpack to avoid getting his feathers wet, and Arthur could feel his warm body curled up against his back.

'It's weird that he doesn't like rain,' said Imogen, who had decided lately – mostly to get a response out of people – that rain was her favourite type of weather. 'You'd think he wouldn't mind it, seeing as he likes to swim.'

'I like swimming,' said Arthur. 'And I don't like the rain.'

'That's because your clothes get wet,' said Imogen.

'Well, Einstein's feathers get wet.'

'His feathers get wet when he swims too.'

'Yes, but he can control it then,' Arthur explained. He often felt that he understood Einstein better than anyone.

The gallery was huge. Great rows of steps led up to the entrance, which was held up by a series of gigantic pillars. It reminded Imogen of the buildings in a book she had once read about Ancient Greece. Trafalgar

Square had emptied out thanks to the rain, and the stone lions were looking sodden and dark, like they'd much rather be inside.

Mr Stewart hissed at Arthur to keep Einstein hidden as they passed a group of museum guides waiting near the doors. Imogen and Arthur followed him closely as he weaved between the crowds and into a room full of landscape paintings, and then another filled with portraits.

Imogen and Arthur raced each other to the benches in each new room they entered, making a game out of it. After a while, Einstein started to get restless.

'It's okay,' Arthur whispered into the zip of his backpack. 'I'll let you out in a minute.'

Imogen agreed to wait for him while he slipped out into the hallway to find the loo. The men's toilet had a couple of people in it – and so, taking a quick look over his shoulder, Arthur slipped into a free baby-changing cubicle and opened up his bag.

He filled the sink with water for Einstein to splash around in.

It was a big, curved sink, and Einstein could very nearly slide on his belly the whole way round the edge. When he had finished playing, Arthur dried him off with the hand-dryer, which made his feathers stand on end like he'd been electrocuted.

'Feeling better now?' asked Arthur, patting his feathers back down with a paper towel.

Just then the door clicked. Arthur froze. He'd forgotten to lock it!

A woman with gingery-grey hair poked her head round the door. 'Whoops, sorry!' she said, spotting Arthur.

He leaped to hide Einstein beneath his coat, and the woman backed out awkwardly.

Arthur's heart thudded in his chest as he tucked Einstein into his bag. He didn't think the woman had noticed anything, but it had been close – too close. He hurried back out into the gallery to find Imogen and Mr Stewart, his stomach doing guilty somersaults at how stupid he had been.

'Right, I suppose you kids would like to go to the gift shop?' said Mr Stewart, as Arthur reappeared.

'I don't really mind,' said Imogen, yawning.

Mr Stewart frowned. 'That's all right,' he said. 'We

can go to the gift shop if you want.'

'I'm a bit tired,' said Arthur.

'Don't you want to see some of those pencils that you like?' asked Mr Stewart, and he strode ahead without waiting for an answer.

Imogen and Arthur shrugged at each other.

They started by admiring some calendars, and then – once they were bored – went over to linger by the exit. On either side of the door were two half-finished-looking statues that showed people's heads from the shoulders up.

Imogen thought they looked like they'd had their heads chopped off – or at least their bodies chopped off from their heads – and wondered whether the lions might have got them. She whispered this rather too loudly to Arthur, and an imperious-looking guide looked down his nose at her.

'They're called busts,' he said. Then, spotting Arthur standing beside her, 'Careful with that backpack, young man,' he added. 'You should be wearing it over one shoulder.'

Einstein had got bigger over the past year, and Arthur was looking visibly weighed down. Imogen had offered more than once to carry his bag, but Arthur wouldn't listen. All this walking round the gallery was starting to make him feel faint.

Arthur nodded and went pink.

'What on earth have you got in it?' the guide continued nosily, but not altogether unpleasantly.

Arthur turned even pinker and looked around for his dad, but Mr Stewart was still in the gift shop, admiring a book of crossword puzzles. Arthur could almost feel his brain stop moving in his head. Penguin, penguin – he couldn't say penguin. What *else* could he possibly have in his bag? He could say anything, anything at all, but the only word he could think of was penguin.

'It's nothing,' said Imogen.

'It's just a picture,' Arthur added, glancing back into the art gallery without thinking.

Imogen stared at him incredulously.

The guide's interest was piqued by that. 'A picture?' he repeated, frowning.

Arthur stared up at him as he slowly realised what he had done.

'It's not a picture,' Imogen said quickly, but that only seemed to make the guide more suspicious.

'You haven't taken anything from the gallery, have you?' he asked. 'Did a grown-up give you that bag and ask you to carry it?'

'It's not a picture,' Arthur agreed. 'I forgot what it was, but I've just remembered. And it definitely isn't a picture.'

'Well, what is it then?'

Arthur searched his mind for the first thing he could think of that sounded heavy. 'Rocks,' he said eventually, in a quiet, half-hearted sort of voice.

'You don't mind if I have a quick peek, do you?' asked the guide, narrowing his eyes.

Imogen glanced into the gift shop at Mr Stewart. Entirely oblivious, he had moved on from the crossword book and was looking very intently at a rack of postcards.

'N-no,' Arthur stammered.

Behind him, a woman was starting to take an interest in the commotion.

Arthur pulled his backpack off his shoulder and placed it on the floor at his feet, straps facing the guide. He looked sheepish as he began, very slowly, to unzip it.

Imogen thought desperately. She wasn't sure what the consequences were for having a penguin in an art gallery, though she didn't much care to find out. She wondered briefly whether there was a special place in museums for confiscated animals, like the box teachers kept confiscated mobile phones in at school.

For a second, Arthur thought he'd felt something touch his leg, but he was probably imagining it – he wasn't thinking straight, after all.

'Here,' he said, tilting his backpack over.

The guide picked up the backpack and peered inside. 'But there's nothing in there,' he said after a moment.

Arthur glanced down. The guide was right: his backpack was empty.

'Fancy playing a prank like that,' the guide went on. 'We don't have all the time in the world, you know. Kids these days need to learn a bit of respect.' He sniffed self-righteously and stalked off in the opposite direction.

As soon as the man was a safe distance away, Imogen grabbed the bag.

'How can he have gone? Wouldn't you have *felt* it if he'd gone?'

'I thought I could feel him there . . .' said Arthur, starting to doubt himself. His neck began to prickle with panic. 'He was right there, and then he wasn't.'

'That's a very clever penguin you've got there.' The woman who had been watching them took a few steps forward and gave a knowing smile.

Imogen and Arthur stared at her.

The woman put her glasses on – strange catlike glasses that had been dangling from her neck – and went over to examine one of the statues.

'He's so still you'd hardly notice him.' She smiled again and her clear blue eyes crinkled at the edges, then she turned and quickly stepped into the gift shop.

Arthur watched her go. It was the same woman he had bumped into in the loo.

He turned to look at the bust she'd been examining,

and then he saw it. Einstein had squeezed himself on to the plinth, and was posing in line with the statue. He was so motionless that he could almost have been part of the set-up: his dark feathers even matched the colour of the stone.

Imogen shrieked with laughter.

'Shh!' said Mr Stewart, finally noticing them and marching over.

Einstein relaxed his pose and looked pleased with himself.

'Einstein!' said Imogen. 'That was amazing!'

'You'd better get back in the bag,' said Arthur a little anxiously, though he was on the verge of laughter too. He held the open backpack up to the plinth, and Einstein plopped into it sideways, as if he was fainting, prompting another shriek of laughter from Imogen.

'What on earth is going on?' said Mr Stewart.

'Nothing,' said Imogen. 'We were just laughing at that statue.'

Mr Stewart looked at it. 'I don't see what's so funny about it,' he said blankly. 'Anyway, I found those pencils that you like . . .'

Chapter Seven

Disaster Strikes

The rest of the day seemed to go very quickly, as weekend days often do. When Arthur went to bed on Sunday night, he still felt happy, but also oddly deprived. It wasn't like Einstein was going anywhere – Arthur knew that – but once they went off to the film set he wouldn't have Einstein to himself any more. It didn't seem fair that other people should get to know Einstein when they didn't really understand him, or care about him like Arthur did.

He watched Einstein roll over at the foot of his bed

and sneeze sleepily into a blanket. Last time Einstein hadn't technically been allowed to sleep upstairs in Arthur's room, but it seemed like this year Mr and Mrs Stewart had lost the heart to ban anything at all.

Gizmo slunk sulkily out of the door to find somewhere to sleep without any penguins.

Still, thought Arthur, at least Einstein would get to see Isaac again. Einstein had probably missed him, and it was Einstein's happiness that mattered in the end, far more than his own.

He wondered where Isaac was going to sleep. Having two penguins at the foot of his bed seemed a bit too many – perhaps they could use the sofa downstairs, and alternate. One night Isaac could sleep downstairs, and the next night Arthur could. He fell asleep, wondering about it still, and dreamed about penguins falling out of his cupboard, and crawling out from underneath his bed, and tumbling from the sky like the rain . . .

*

'Get back!' the cameraman shouted. 'You're moving into the shot.'

He turned to Bill Hunter, who was sitting cross-legged on a foldaway chair, playing a game on his phone.

'Will the penguins be okay to do that shot again, Bill?'

'Sure, sure, take it from the top,' said Bill Hunter vaguely.

'Shouldn't he be more interested?' whispered Imogen.

Arthur shrugged and looked baffled.

Mr and Mrs Stewart had driven them over after school to see how everything was going. They had never been on a set before, and Imogen found it fascinating. She hadn't imagined so many people would be involved. A short, round man was holding up a stick with a fluffy sort of ball on the end – she guessed that it must be a microphone. Several people were clustered round the camera, moving it this way and that on miniature railway tracks. And every few minutes a well-dressed woman would come bustling over from the corner to readjust Einstein's feathers and comb Isaac's eyebrows back into place.

Imogen stared around in amazement, then looked at Bill Hunter in confusion. She wished she had his job. She was fairly sure she'd be much better at it.

Arthur was more interested in watching Einstein who – to his relief – looked perfectly happy. *That* was one thing Arthur didn't think he would ever understand about Einstein: how much he liked attention. In fact, Arthur was becoming increasingly sure that Einstein was messing up his feathers on purpose, just so the woman would rush over and comb them again.

'Doesn't he look brilliant!' said Mrs Stewart. 'Everyone's going to want to hire him now!'

Bill Hunter glanced up at the sound of Mrs Stewart's

voice, and his whole demeanour changed. Suddenly he was on his feet, marching over to shake the Stewarts by the hand. He even bent down to shake Imogen and Arthur's hands too.

'I'm so glad you made it,' he said. 'It's been a hectic day, but we're definitely making progress. Come, let me give you a tour.'

He led them into the middle of the studio and started talking about how expensive the equipment was.

Imogen watched the slow curve of his mouth move and didn't listen to a word he was saying. She couldn't understand how he managed to smile constantly yet look so serious at the same time.

He glanced down, catching her gaze, and a filling in one of his teeth flashed gold. 'Wouldn't you agree?' he asked.

Imogen blinked at him. 'What?'

Bill Hunter laughed charmingly and ruffled her hair. 'Kids, eh?' he said, and led them over to where Einstein and Isaac were standing in front of a big green screen.

Imogen held back, frowning, as she tried to return her hair to its original position. She wished the make-up woman would come and comb her too.

Ahead of her, Bill Hunter had started gesturing busily at the penguins. 'Marvellous performance from Isaac this morning, I must say.'

'We haven't actually filmed Isaac's entrance yet,' the cameraman pointed out.

Just then Einstein spotted Arthur and Imogen and squawked hello. They both waved back enthusiastically.

'Don't worry!' called Arthur. 'It's nearly home time!'

'I wouldn't be so sure,' Bill Hunter muttered.

Imogen looked up at him. 'What did you say?' she asked.

He shrugged innocently. 'We work long hours around here. But that's showbiz for you.' Then he picked up his phone and tapped something into it.

All of a sudden the lights in the studio cut out, and the room was plunged into darkness. A chorus of confused voices filled the air.

'What happened there?' someone called.

A door creaked and clattered shut. Something fell on to the floor. In the distance a penguin squawked.

'Imogen, where are you?' said Arthur. He reached out and touched her coat.

'I'm here,' replied Imogen, squeezing his hand and doing her best to squint through the darkness, but of course there weren't any windows in the studio, so a power cut meant total darkness. Not even shadows.

'It's nothing,' she told him. 'Just a power cut.'

'I'll turn my camera flash on while someone finds the fuse,' the cameraman suggested.

In the bright white light that cut across the studio Imogen swore she could see someone moving, someone near Einstein, someone who hadn't been there before.

'No, don't waste the battery,' said Bill Hunter, and the white light disappeared. 'I can fix it myself.'

Imogen stood for a moment in confusion, then started to fumble her way over to the green screen. Something was wrong – she could feel it now. If only she could find her way past all this equipment . . . But before she had time to think the lights had turned back on again, and she was blinking in the sudden brightness.

'What was that all about?' another person called out.

'Just a technical fault, I should imagine,' said Mr Stewart, to no one in particular.

'Einstein!' cried Imogen.

Arthur turned to the green screen. The space where Einstein and Isaac had been standing just a moment ago was empty, and the door a few metres behind it was swaying imperceptibly on its hinges.

'They've gone!'

'*What?*' Bill Hunter's voice cut authoritatively through the crowd. 'They can't have gone – don't be ridiculous.' He marched over and stared at the floor, as if it could have swallowed them up somehow.

'What's that by your foot?' cried Mrs Stewart. 'There's a note!'

Bill Hunter bent down to pick the piece of paper up. ***'I have the penguins. I am holding them hostage,'*** he read, then gasped theatrically.

Arthur stared at him. In the chaos of voices that followed he had the strange sense that he was still dreaming.

'They must have gone out of that door!' cried

Imogen, and in a burst of determination she pushed past Bill Hunter and dived through it, finding herself in one of the strange abandoned corridors.

She tried running to the left for a few metres, then turned round and ran to the right. On either side of her stretched a long white floor. It was empty. Her heart sank. They were already gone.

That was when she spotted something on the floor in front of her and knelt down to pick it up.

It was a pair of glasses. Narrow, catlike ones, with a little chain attached. They had been crushed slightly on one side, and caught up in one of the hinges was the tiniest fleck of feather.

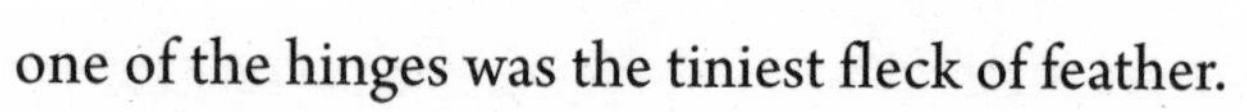

Imogen paused, then tucked the glasses into her pocket. Something told her not to mention them to anyone, particularly not to Bill Hunter. Slowly she pushed open the door to the studio and saw that he was already clambering on to a chair to make a speech.

'Nobody must panic,' he insisted. 'Not all of you know this, but I am, in fact, a qualified detective. This is precisely the sort of situation I have undergone rigorous training for. And I can assure you – all of you – that I *will* find Einstein and Isaiah and return them safely.'

'Isaac,' Imogen corrected crossly from behind him.

Bill Hunter swivelled round to smile at her. 'That's what I said.'

'And I'm a detective too,' said Imogen. She looked at Arthur, talking to him more than anyone. 'Don't worry. I'll find them.'

Bill Hunter chuckled. 'You just leave it to me,' he said. 'You had your moment in the spotlight, but it's best to let the professionals handle it this time. I imagine you have plenty of homework to be getting on with, don't you, Imogen?'

*

'It doesn't make sense,' whispered Imogen. She slapped the palm of her hand against her forehead and scowled.

The policeman was jotting down notes in his notebook as Mr and Mrs Stewart fought over each other to explain what had happened. Bill Hunter stood a few metres away from them, looking serious yet oddly serene.

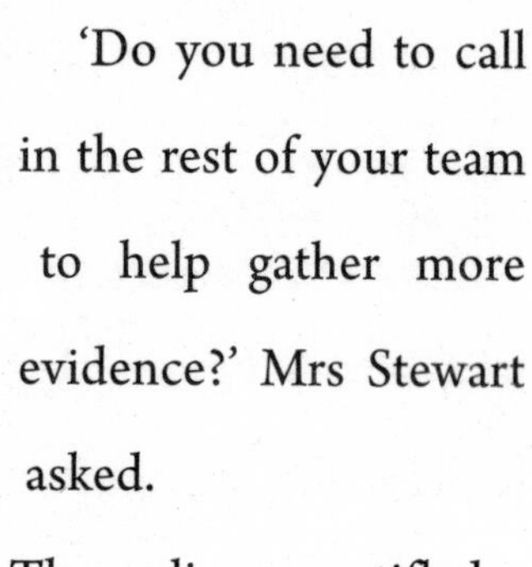

'Do you need to call in the rest of your team to help gather more evidence?' Mrs Stewart asked.

The policeman stifled a yawn with the edge of his hand, then scratched his bottom. 'Animal cases like this, ma'am, they don't often lead anywhere.'

'What do you mean they don't lead anywhere?' said Mr Stewart.

'I'm not surprised they don't with an attitude like that!' Mrs Stewart snapped.

The policeman looked crestfallen. 'Obviously we'll keep an eye out and everything,' he mumbled.

'I have the situation under control,' Bill Hunter interrupted. He was glancing philosophically out of the window, and didn't bother turning round to address them. 'Just give me some time.'

'Last time you had a situation under control you got half eaten by a miniature penguin!' said Mrs Stewart, immediately looking embarrassed at having spoken to anyone so harshly.

Bill Hunter gave a condescending little smile and opened his mouth to reply. Suddenly Imogen couldn't help herself.

'It was him!' she cried, pointing at Bill Hunter. 'You have to arrest him!'

The policeman turned to look at her. 'You mean this gentleman in the long white coat?'

'Yes!' said Imogen. 'Who else would have done it?'

The policeman scratched his head and looked down at his notebook. 'According to witness accounts, miss, this gentleman was *in* the studio at precisely the same time the kidnapper was running *out* of the studio. He'd have to have been in two places at once.'

'That's right, little Imogen,' said Bill Hunter. 'It can't have been me. I have an albino.'

'An *alibi*,' Imogen corrected.

'That's what I said.'

Imogen glowered at him. 'I don't know how you did it, but I know that it was you! *And* I'm going to prove it!'

'Imogen,' Mrs Stewart scolded. 'Of course it wasn't Mr Hunter. Why on earth would he want to kidnap Einstein and Isaac when he's using them in his advert?'

Imogen stared at her mother in confusion. She

hadn't seemed to like Bill Hunter a moment ago, so why was she taking his side all of a sudden?

'We can't all keep falling out,' Mrs Stewart went on. 'We need to work together to help this policeman find out what *really* happened.'

'Like I said, ma'am, these animal cases . . .' muttered the policeman.

Imogen gritted her teeth in frustration and ran to find her brother.

Chapter Eight

A Confiscation

'Arthur!' Theo shouted across the playground and came rushing over to greet his friend.

Arthur's stomach did a somersault. For some reason, he didn't *want* to see Theo. All of last week he'd been telling Theo about Einstein coming back. His return was all they had spoken about yesterday during lunch.

He hadn't even mentioned his worries, the ones he'd been having about Bill Hunter and whether he was trustworthy. Somehow explaining his concerns to

Theo would have made them feel real, but now they *were* real – horribly, completely real. And what had Arthur done to prevent it all? Nothing.

'Have you got him?' asked Theo. 'Can I see? Show me!'

Yesterday Arthur had made the mistake of promising Theo that he would bring Einstein to school soon. The penguins were meant to have days off from filming; he just hadn't known when they were going to be. Now he didn't suppose he'd ever know.

Instead, Arthur pulled on the straps of his backpack and felt its weightlessness. He had half hoped that Einstein would reappear, that something would pull him out of this nightmare, and he would unzip his bag to find Einstein blinking up at him, ready to help him with his maths. But all he heard was the gentle flop of his pencil case rolling from one side of the backpack to the other, touching nothing.

Theo looked concerned. 'What is it?'

‘He’s gone,’ Arthur whispered. ‘Somebody took him.’

‘What do you mean?’ said Theo. ‘Yesterday you said that he was here. Didn’t you spend the whole weekend with him?’

‘We went to see him after school,’ Arthur explained. ‘And somebody took him.’ His voice wobbled a little. Then he gave in and told Theo everything.

Imogen put her hand inside her jacket and felt the reading glasses. She had kept them tucked away ever since finding them in the studio yesterday. She hadn’t even shown them to her family: Mr and Mrs Stewart might want to hand them in as evidence to the policeman, but Imogen knew – or at least she strongly suspected – that they weren’t going to be of any use in *his* hands. And as for Arthur – well, she had become caught up in the case, and she didn’t suppose it was unusual for detectives to work alone. Perhaps she'd tell him later.

She ran her fingers along their textured frame, and touched the little chain that dangled from the side. As she did so, her mind started to whir and race, and the sound of her history teacher's voice sank into a low drawl, then disappeared completely.

Who might the glasses belong to? She couldn't remember anyone wearing them inside the studio, and she was positive that they weren't Bill Hunter's. No, Imogen knew what he looked like – she had always kept a very clear picture of him in her head – and he definitely didn't wear glasses, least of all ones like *this.*

It did seem odd, she supposed, that Bill Hunter had been standing right next to her during the kidnapping. Of course, the lights had gone out, and she hadn't actually been able to see him – but it would have been very difficult for him to rush the penguins away to a hiding place and return not even out of breath, all in the space of a minute. To be perfectly honest, Imogen didn't think he was up to it.

And yet she was so sure – or at least she'd *felt* so sure yesterday – that Bill Hunter had to be at the heart of it all. Her mind drifted back to Arthur a few days ago, telling her not to trust him, and her stomach twisted into a heavy, guilty knot. She had been too excited to listen, too happy to look at the evidence properly. That didn't make her much of a detective, did it?

What had the note said? *I have the penguins. I am holding them hostage.*

Imogen pulled her detective notebook out of her school bag to double-check. She had written everything down in it last night, while it was still fresh in her head: the wording of the note, the things people had said, even the time at which the policeman had scratched his bottom. Her eyes skimmed over her own handwriting. Then, with her teacher's voice still a distant hum from over by the whiteboard, she started to doodle.

'Hey, Imogen. What are you drawing?'

Alfie, a boy she didn't much like, pulled Imogen out of her daydream from the desk behind her.

'Is that a penguin?'

Imogen looked down at her notebook. She supposed that it was a penguin, although it didn't really look like one. Its head was too small.

Amy Diggory gave a giggle from the next desk along. Amy had been one of Imogen's best friends until a few weeks ago, but now she'd started sitting next to Gracie, the new girl, and never bothered to wait for Imogen after lunch.

Imogen wasn't sure why. She didn't think she had done anything. Amy used to like the same things she liked, but now she was into the same things Gracie was, and made a point of it. The weird thing was that Imogen didn't even dislike Gracie. She'd have been perfectly happy to be friends with both of them.

'Imogen has a pet penguin, didn't you know?' Amy whispered loudly, then started giggling again.

Imogen calmly tore a page out of her notebook, screwed it up into a ball and threw it at the back of Amy's head.

'I'll take that,' said Mr Daunt, marching over to scoop Imogen's notebook up off the desk. 'You can have it back on Monday.'

Chapter Nine

Einstein's Prison

Einstein blinked at the dim puddle of light that had come tumbling into the room as the day broke. There was only one window: a skylight squeezed into the corner of the ceiling, revealing the shifting branches of a tree and the spiky edge of a TV aerial.

The rain hadn't let up all night, and it was drumming rhythmically through a grey sunrise.

A metre or so away, Isaac was fast asleep still, his head drooping heavily against his chest. Einstein, however, gave every appearance of being wide awake.

His eyes darted round the room, from the chair in the corner, to the dying plant beneath the window, to the boxes stacked precariously on the floor around it . . .

He looked just on the edge of a thought when the door thudded open, and somebody marched in. Somebody tall, somebody with gingery-grey hair. A woman. She was wearing an ugly pink cardigan and squinting awkwardly.

Einstein gave her an irritated look, but he didn't seem surprised.

'Morning, penguins,' she crooned and went to sit in the chair as Isaac shook himself awake and squawked at her.

'Don't talk to me like that,' she warned him and began sifting through a large pile of paperwork.

A few seconds later, she stood up to

turn the lights on, and the chair creaked underneath her as she returned to it. She pulled a piece of paper closer to her face and squinted at it, then gave up and started picking the dirt out from underneath her fingernails instead.

'What?' she said, noticing Einstein staring at her. 'My new glasses haven't arrived yet.'

'Stupid penguin,' she muttered when Einstein didn't move. 'You don't understand a word I'm saying.'

Einstein went on staring at her.

'Boo!' she told him.

But Einstein couldn't help it. All of a sudden, he was starting to realise why she looked familiar. He had seen her before, hadn't he? At the weekend, with Arthur . . .

Suddenly the woman's phone rang. 'Hello? Bill?' she said. 'Yes, darling, it's me.' She tucked her greying hair behind her ear and wandered over to the door. 'Sorry, I can't hear you over the sound of that penguin snoring.'

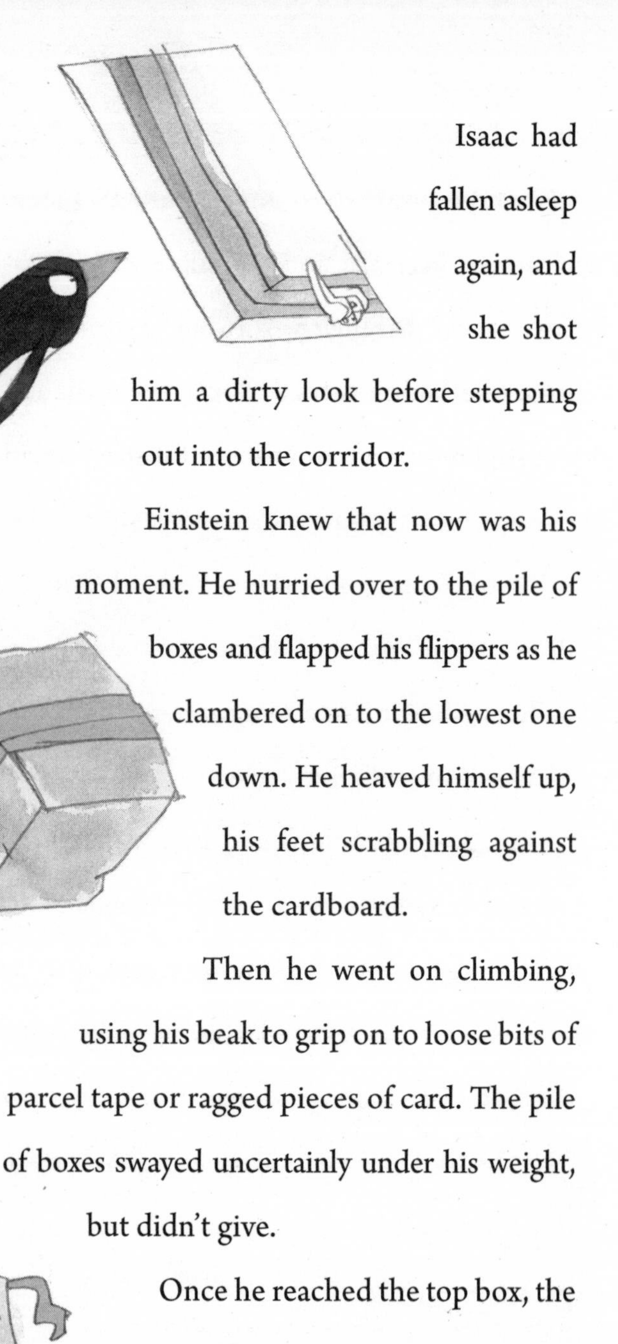

Isaac had fallen asleep again, and she shot him a dirty look before stepping out into the corridor.

Einstein knew that now was his moment. He hurried over to the pile of boxes and flapped his flippers as he clambered on to the lowest one down. He heaved himself up, his feet scrabbling against the cardboard.

Then he went on climbing, using his beak to grip on to loose bits of parcel tape or ragged pieces of card. The pile of boxes swayed uncertainly under his weight, but didn't give.

Once he reached the top box, the

window was just one big leap into the air above him.

Einstein wished that it wasn't raining. Last night the woman had left the window open to let some air in, but she'd closed it again by the time she left the room. She hadn't actually locked it – thanks to her short-sightedness, perhaps – but it still looked heavy. He was just going to have to try his luck. He bent his knees and jumped . . .

. . . and crashed into the glass with a loud *thwack*.

The window flew open. Isaac woke up and squawked in shock.

But by then Einstein was falling again, tumbling down, down, down into the plant pot below. It collapsed on to the floor with a clatter, spilling soil everywhere, and high up above him Einstein saw the

window sway on its hinges for a moment before banging shut under its own weight.

The woman came rushing back inside, but this time someone else came rushing in behind her.

Bill Hunter stood over Einstein and leered at him.

'Well, well, well, what have we here?' he said. 'A runaway penguin? Or should I say a flyaway penguin?'

He paused to laugh at his own joke, then bent down to pull Einstein back on to his feet.

'We can't have runaway penguins, I'm afraid. But there's nothing to fret about, Einstein. I think you'll find we're going to become friends.'

In the corner the woman was starting to tidy up the boxes, pushing them away from the window – much further away than they'd been before, too far away for Einstein to try again. He watched her anxiously.

'Besides,' Bill Hunter went on, 'we can't have you escaping and wandering the streets alone. There are bad people out there. You might get kidnapped!'

Isaac took a few steps forward and gave an angry squawk.

'Enough of that,' Bill Hunter snapped back. 'I'm not sure I like the one with the yellow eyebrows,' he remarked to the woman. Then, '*Ow!*' he cried.

Einstein had bitten him on the hand again, leaving a nasty red mark across his fingers.

Chapter Ten

Bill Hunter Comes to Visit

Imogen stared into the bottom of her mug. A few specks of chocolate had stuck to the sides.

She was tired. Washed up. One more lowlife hoodlum making her life a slow-motion misery and she might just go to bed without brushing her teeth.

'Are you all right, dear?' Mrs Stewart asked.

Imogen pushed the mug towards her mother. 'Pour me another, will you?' she muttered. 'And don't go so easy on the chocolate this time.'

'Oh, Imogen,' Mrs Stewart sighed. 'We went over

this yesterday. You're going to get your notebook back on Monday.' But she took the mug and topped it up all the same.

'It's not about the notebook!' said Imogen. 'It's about what's *in* the notebook!'

'We're going to find Einstein and Isaac. Your dad and I are as worried as you are – we've been talking to the police all day. They'll work it out. It is their job, after all.'

'No one's going to work it out if I don't get my notebook back!' Imogen insisted. 'I had *everything* in there. I just needed to put it all together . . .'

'You're a very good detective, Imogen,' said Mrs Stewart kindly.

'You wouldn't say it in that voice if you really meant it,' Imogen mumbled.

Just then the doorbell rang, and Arthur hopped up from the sofa to answer it. He had been listening to their conversation from the living room, and it had worried him. Was Imogen right? Was the notebook really that important? And, if it was, could they afford to wait until Monday to get it back?

As he wandered into the hallway, he imagined himself abseiling down the vertical face of the school, his sister's notebook in his teeth, as a crowd of unspecified people cheered him from the playground below.

He had half

forgotten what he was doing when he jumped at the sight of Bill Hunter on the doorstep.

'Arthur!' Bill Hunter cried, bending down to ruffle his hair. 'How are you, kid? Having fun? Playing football?'

Arthur blinked at him. 'Er . . . No.'

Mrs Stewart poked her head round the kitchen door. 'Oh, Bill!' she said. 'What a surprise. Is everything all right?'

'Of course,' said Bill. 'Never better. I just thought I'd pop round and see how these young scallywags are doing.'

'Right . . .' Mrs Stewart looked confused. 'Well, you'd better come in.'

Arthur stepped to one side and watched Bill Hunter swoop into the hallway, tossing his coat in the general direction of a hook and not noticing when it missed and landed on the floor. He helped himself to a seat at the kitchen table while Mrs Stewart hurriedly cleared her work from around him.

'Hello, Imogen!' said Bill Hunter. 'How are you doing?'

Imogen stared at him. Last time they'd seen each other she had accused him of kidnapping someone. 'Fine,' she said blankly.

'Only *fine*? You should be running around, enjoying the sunshine!'

'It isn't sunny,' Imogen pointed out. 'And I'm worried.'

'Worried!' cried Bill Hunter. 'About what? A spelling test?'

'About Einstein!'

'Ah, yes,' he said gravely. 'Well, I wouldn't fret about that.'

'He's been missing for two days! Of course I'm worried.'

'I'm certain that I am on the *cusp* of finding him. That's what I came here to tell you, in fact.'

'You are?' said Mrs Stewart. She had looked cautious at first, but quickly became excited. 'Well, that's good news, isn't it, kids?'

'Ah, hello,' said Mr Stewart from the stairs. 'I thought I heard voices.'

'James, Bill says he's nearly found Einstein and Isaac. Isn't that good?'

Mr Stewart paused. 'You have?' he said stiffly. 'I've been on the phone about it all day. Got a few decent theories myself.'

He shuffled over to the kettle to make the tea.

'So where are they?' asked Imogen.

'What do you mean?' said Bill Hunter. 'I haven't found them *yet*.'

'But if you think you've nearly found them then you must have some ideas about it.'

'Of course I do.'

'So what are they?'

Bill Hunter considered this. 'Well, the thing is to

examine the evidence closely and then apply it to the bigger picture.'

The Stewarts all looked at him expectantly. Imogen slurped her hot chocolate and narrowed her eyes.

'The truth is I have several theories,' Bill Hunter declared, in a fit of inspiration. 'You see, the first . . . the first is that they ran away!'

'Einstein didn't *run away*!' cried Arthur.

'Troubled penguins can surprise you.'

'How would he have opened the door by himself?' asked Imogen. 'He doesn't have opposable thumbs. Or hands.'

Bill Hunter frowned. 'Well, as I said, that one is my least favourite theory.'

'You didn't say that.'

'The second theory,' he went on, bending and unbending his thumbs experimentally under the table, 'is that they were kidnapped.'

'We already *know* that,' Imogen said. 'We're trying to work out *who by*.'

'All right, let's not be rude,' warned Mrs Stewart.

'After all, the note said *I am holding the penguins hostage,* which suggests that somebody has the penguins, and is holding them—'

'*I have the penguins. I am holding them hostage,*' Imogen found herself mumbling aloud. Mrs Stewart usually told her off for correcting people, but in this case she couldn't help it.

'What?' said Bill Hunter.

'That's what the note said. It was two sentences, not one.'

Bill Hunter smiled at this. He reached into his pocket and smugly slapped the note down on to the table in front of her. Imogen picked it up and looked at it. *I am holding the penguins hostage,* it said, in shaky black handwriting.

'Not so smart now, are we?'

Imogen blinked. That couldn't be right . . . She could have sworn . . .

'How do you like your tea?' asked Mr Stewart, placing several mugs down on the table.

'Milk and sugar, please.'

'I'll let you do it.'

Bill Hunter tipped the sugar in his mug, then attempted to hand the pot back to Mr Stewart.

'No, thanks,' said Mr Stewart pointedly. 'I prefer mine strong.'

'I don't think you have any ideas about any of it at all,' said Imogen decidedly.

'I have a good deal more than you do,' Bill Hunter snapped. 'I don't want to compromise the mission by revealing my secrets.'

'Then why did you come here?'

'*Imogen,*' Mrs Stewart said crossly, though Mr Stewart looked a little proud.

'Well,' said Bill Hunter after a few sips of tea, 'I suppose I'd better leave. I can tell I'm not wanted. But I just came to share the good news.'

'Oh, Bill. Finish your tea first,' said Mrs Stewart sympathetically. She wasn't very good at not feeling sorry for people when she needed to.

'When do you think you'll have found them by?' asked Arthur.

He wasn't quite sure whether he was interrogating the man, like Imogen was, or asking the question hopefully. It seemed to come out forcefully and then turn genuine halfway through.

'Oh – by Friday evening, I should think.'

Imogen watched Bill Hunter as he finished his tea, and she was still watching him when he walked into the hallway to find his coat. She even stood up to follow him.

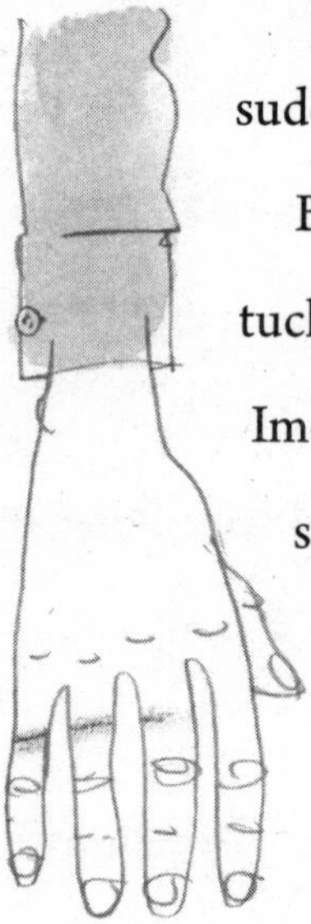

'What's that on your hand?' she asked suddenly.

Bill Hunter looked surprised and quickly tucked his hand into his pocket, but Imogen had already seen it: the nasty red stripe across his fingers. In the shape of a penguin's beak.

'What's what on my hand?' asked Bill innocently.

'It's in your pocket now.'

He took his left hand out of his pocket and waved it around in the light.

'Your other hand.'

'Oh, that?'

Even Mr and Mrs Stewart, peering through from the kitchen, were looking interested now.

'That's where Einstein bit me the other day at the airport.'

'Gosh,' said Mrs Stewart, 'and it's still red? You should put some ice on that.'

When Imogen went to bed that night, her mind was racing. Little bits of evidence were spinning round her head, and now that it was quiet she could almost feel them slotting together, making sense of things that hadn't made sense before.

That mark on Bill Hunter's hand . . . It was raw, like it hadn't been there long. And, although she couldn't remember perfectly, Imogen didn't think it had been there at the studio film set on Monday.

And, as for the note, she *knew* she hadn't been wrong. She had written down exactly what Bill Hunter had read out on Monday in her notebook, word for word. *Which suggested,* Imogen thought to herself, frowning, *that he had read the note out incorrectly at the time.* It seemed strange that he would read it out so carelessly when it was so important and he'd never seen it before . . .

Or perhaps he *had* seen it before. Perhaps his carelessness came from overconfidence that he didn't need to reread it. And did that – could that – mean that he had actually *written* it? If only she had her notebook to confirm her suspicions!

After all, he was acting so sure of himself! How could he be so confident about things if he didn't know more than he was giving away? Friday evening was a very specific deadline, and how could he be so certain . . .?

'Don't worry, Einstein,' Imogen whispered, frowning determinedly at herself in the mirror as she brushed her teeth. 'I'll prove that it was him.'

What she didn't understand, of course, was why. *Why* would he want to kidnap Einstein and Isaac when he needed them for his work? It would make sense if he was planning on keeping them, or selling them, but he'd been talking as if he was actually planning on giving them back.

Slowly she pulled the note out of her pocket. Bill Hunter had forgotten to pick it up off the kitchen table. She read the word **hostage**. Wasn't the point of having a hostage that you asked for something to secure their safe return? But no one had asked for anything. There was still something missing, something that didn't make sense yet.

Imogen wandered back into her bedroom and sat behind the curtains on the windowsill. The sky all around her was the dark, deep colour of ink – more blue than black – and glowing at the edges. She wondered whether Einstein was still underneath it, whether perhaps he was looking up at it now too.

There were never any stars in London, although the moon was bright enough, and the streetlights did a good job of holding back the darkness. Once or twice Imogen thought she saw a star peeking out from among the clouds and smog, but they always disappeared too quickly, swallowed back into the waters of the London night.

The flickering light of an aeroplane went sliding by, and Imogen, pretending to herself that it was a shooting star, after all, made a small wish under her breath.

Not so far across the same city Einstein rolled over in his sleep. He could almost hear her.

Chapter Eleven

The Notebook Heist

Imogen had already explained the plan three times by the time they reached the school gates.

'Are you sure you don't want me to do it?' she asked, putting a nervous hand on Arthur's shoulder.

Arthur shrugged her off irritatedly. 'You *need* me to do it,' he reminded her.

'Make sure no one sees you,' she said. 'But, if they do, you can tell them that you were looking for the computer room, and you got lost.'

'We *know*,' said Arthur, barely hiding his exasperation.

She had even made him sign up for the breaktime computer course: the computer room was in the same building as the history classroom her notebook was being kept in, and it would make a good excuse if he was questioned. Arthur didn't much like the idea of being caught and having to spend half an hour pretending to be interested in spreadsheets, but he supposed that it was for the greater good.

'We'll be fine,' added Theo, who had already volunteered to help. 'How hard can it be?'

'Okay,' said Imogen. 'Well, let me know how it goes.'

She watched gloomily as Arthur and Theo walked away across the playground. She wouldn't be able to concentrate, leaving something up to her brother like that. What if he lost the notebook forever? What if he got caught? She'd have done it herself, but if Mr Daunt found her sneaking around in his classroom he'd know exactly what she was up to. At least the boys were in with a chance of pulling it off.

'Hi!'

It was Gracie, greeting Imogen as she walked past.

To Gracie's left, Amy pursed her lips and gave Imogen a brief glare, then quickly looked away again.

Imogen blinked after them in surprise. 'Hi,' she said, largely to their backs, then went over to join some of the other girls on their way into the classroom.

'Is everything okay?' asked Theo.

Arthur had started going quiet over lunch, which wasn't exactly abnormal, but he had been even quieter than usual. At first it had been out of sadness: he was worrying about Einstein as he pushed his baked beans in circles round the edge of his plate. But, shortly after the beans had turned to mush and disappeared underneath his uneaten broccoli, his sadness had turned into a sort of silent determination – a feeling Arthur wasn't entirely used to.

Arthur nodded to show that he was fine. They were nearly at the right building now – the one Imogen had directed them to. It was the oldest part of the school, with big, looming red walls and a roof that made it look like it was frowning.

Arthur had only been inside it once or twice before. Most of the time those classrooms were for the older children, like Imogen, and Arthur didn't often like going into new places. But today he didn't think he felt nervous at all.

Occasionally a nerve would rear its head and try drifting up to the surface, but he would ignore it.

'Let's get that notebook back,' said Arthur, pushing open the door.

It was quiet inside, and as the door slammed shut the voices of the other children in the playground outside faded to a distant babble. Arthur could hear his feet echoing loudly on the stairs.

'Shouldn't we tiptoe?' whispered Theo.

Arthur shook his head. 'We don't want to look suspicious.'

Just then a teacher rounded the corner of the stairs ahead of them. It wasn't a teacher Arthur knew, but one he recognised from assembly: he looked tall and old and serious, with big eyes and a large, sensible nose.

Arthur held his breath.

'Afternoon, boys,' said the teacher nonchalantly. He was swinging a keyring around between his fingers.

Arthur and Theo mumbled awkwardly back at him, and the teacher carried on walking, disappearing down into the same stairwell they had emerged from.

'I think that was him,' whispered Arthur.

'Who? Mr Daunt?'

'Yes!' said Arthur excitedly. 'That means his classroom will be empty!'

They hurried up to the very top of the building. Arthur couldn't believe how easy this was turning out to be.

He put his face up to the window in the classroom door and peered inside. Yes, it was empty. Rows of desks sat waiting with no one beside them, and Arthur pushed the door.

Nothing happened.

Arthur frowned, then pushed the door again. He could feel it move slightly, but all he heard was the muffled thud of the door's lock against its frame as it refused to open.

'Oh, no,' whispered Theo. 'It's locked.'

Arthur's eyes widened as he rushed to the stairwell window. 'He has the keys in his hands!'

Mr Daunt had left the building and was strolling in the direction of the staffroom, his keyring still swinging between his fingers. Arthur watched him through the dirty glass like he was watching a character on a TV screen.

After a few moments, Arthur turned and looked at his friend. He felt like running back to the playground and telling Imogen, letting her deal with it, or at least putting it off until tomorrow. But then he thought about Einstein, and about Isaac, and it almost seemed to Arthur as if it was *them* who were locked up and confiscated in Mr Daunt's classroom – so close, but just out of reach. All of a sudden, the idea of waiting any longer seemed impossible.

Arthur took a deep breath. 'Let's follow him.'

'Mr Daunt!' cried Theo.

The tall teacher turned round and glanced down at them. He was most of the way across the playground now, nearly at the staffroom, and he looked a little taken aback at being disturbed.

'Yes?'

'We were looking for you.'

Mr Daunt frowned. 'Weren't you just on the way up to my classroom?'

'Yes,' said Arthur. 'But we weren't sure whether it was really you.'

'How can I help you?' he asked, in a voice that didn't suggest he was very interested in helping.

Theo looked at Arthur in a panic. 'Well . . . er . . .' he mumbled, searching for words.

'We've heard about you, and we wanted to ask you some questions,' said Arthur, glancing back at Theo significantly.

'Questions about what?'

'About history!' said Arthur. 'We were told you know more about history than anyone else in the school.'

'Than anyone else in London,' Theo added.

Mr Daunt gave them a satisfied, thoughtful sort of look. 'Yes, well, I do know *quite* a bit . . .'

'And we're very interested in doing a project on the history of the school,' said Arthur. 'Just for fun. We were wondering if you could help us?'

By now, Mr Daunt was positively glowing. He

jangled his keys and absent-mindedly dropped them into his jacket pocket. 'You were?'

'Yes!' said Arthur hurriedly. He half turned to Theo and tried to indicate Mr Daunt's pocket with his eyes, then asked the first question he could think of. 'How long have you worked here?'

'Me? Well, I've been here for thirty years. It looked very different when I started, of course. There weren't as many buildings, and this playground didn't exist yet . . .'

Arthur tried his best to look interested, only occasionally allowing his eyes to drift towards Theo, who was sidling closer to Mr Daunt's jacket as he droned dreamily on.

'The school lunches were particularly bad back then. There's some information on that in the archives. I could print it out for you if you like?'

Theo was almost there, but Mr Daunt's arm was in the way.

'Which building was the oldest?' asked Arthur suddenly.

'The one behind you.'

'Which one?' said Arthur. 'I can't see it.'

'What do you mean you can't see it? It's right behind you.'

'Can you point it out for me?'

Mr Daunt pointed, and in the brief moment that his arm was in the air

Theo shoved his hand inside the jacket pocket and lifted out the keys.

'*Oh*,' said Arthur. 'I didn't realise you meant *that* building. I think I'll go and have a look at it. Thank you for everything!'

Mr Daunt looked puzzled and, in a daze, turned round to continue on his way to the staffroom.

As they hurried back up the stairs to Mr Daunt's classroom, Arthur didn't think he had ever felt his heart beat so quickly. At first it alarmed him, but after a moment he realised that it wasn't a bad sort of fast. He actually felt excited doing something he wasn't supposed to be doing. He'd have broken all the rules in the world to rescue Einstein.

'Do you think he noticed?' he panted.

'No, he was too busy going on about history,' said Theo. 'And anyway he kept walking towards the staffroom.'

Theo reached into his pocket and pulled out the bunch of keys. The third key they tried slipped neatly into the lock, and the door clicked open.

Arthur almost had to stop himself from doing a victory dance as he stepped inside. *Focus,* he told himself. *You might still get caught,* though he was feeling much too pleased with himself to be particularly bothered by the idea.

Theo kept watch at the door while Arthur rifled through the drawers of Mr Daunt's desk. Most of them were full of old whiteboard pens, or books that were peeling apart at the spine and looked like they might crumble into dust if somebody touched them. Then Arthur spotted the bottom drawer labelled Confiscations.

'Got it!' Arthur cried.

Imogen's notebook was sitting at the very top, along with several old toys, a bag of sweets and a pack of cards. Arthur picked up the notebook and shoved it into his pocket, paused for a moment, then picked the sweets up too.

*

'What are you doing?' whispered Theo a short while later, when they were safely sitting down in their French lesson.

Arthur had pulled the notebook out of his backpack and was flicking through it beneath the desk.

'You're going to get it confiscated again,' said Theo.

Arthur hissed at him to be quiet, then offered him a sweet from the bag he had stolen by way of apology. But he couldn't put the notebook down.

Imogen really had written *everything*. Arthur didn't think there was a detail she had missed, from the timings of the events to where the doors had been positioned in the studio. She had even made a note of the colour of the policeman's shoes. And her writing had become so neat over the last year too that it really was something to look at.

In fact, Arthur was so impressed that he started to feel a little put out at the fact that Imogen hadn't shared her notebook with him before. He had good ideas too, didn't he? He'd been the first to worry about the dangers of Einstein's return – and, while he supposed it was still possible that he'd been wrong to worry about Bill Hunter specifically, he certainly hadn't been wrong to be concerned. He felt he had a right to have his opinion taken seriously.

Arthur turned the page. Here Imogen had drawn a diagram of a pair of narrow reading glasses with a thin chain attached to each side. Arthur frowned and looked more closely. Why had she done that?

GLASSES FOUND IN STUDIO CORRIDOR ALONG WITH FEATHER

He turned the page, hoping to find out whose glasses they were, but to his surprise it was at that point that Imogen's curly handwriting stopped.

Perhaps she didn't know whose glasses they were.

Imogen not knowing something – now that was a strange thought.

'*La robe rouge*,' said the French teacher from over by the whiteboard.

'The red dress,' the class chanted after her, and Arthur quickly looked up and mumbled along with them. Last lesson they had learned about colours, and now they'd moved on to items of clothing.

'*Les lunettes*,' said the teacher.

'The glasses,' said the class.

'*Une chemise*,' said the teacher, lifting up a card with a picture of a shirt on, but by then Arthur had stopped listening. The words 'red' and 'glasses' were swirling around in his head, as if his brain was trying to connect them somehow but wasn't sure why.

Then all at once it came to him: the woman in the National Gallery last weekend, the one with the red hair. *She* had worn glasses. And, what's more, her glasses had a chain holding them in place – exactly like the one Imogen had drawn – and she had seemed very interested in Einstein.

Arthur could scarcely believe what his brain was telling him. Was it possible? Could that woman have been following them?

'Are you going to come to my birthday party?' asked Amy, and Imogen turned at the sound of her voice.

But of course it wasn't Imogen that Amy was talking to. It was another group of girls from their class.

Imogen's stomach sank. Up until last year, she and Amy had always done their birthday parties together. Their shared birthday had been what started the friendship, but that was a long time ago now – before Gracie arrived.

With all the fuss about Einstein, Imogen had hardly started to think about inviting friends over for her birthday. Now she didn't suppose there would be any left to go around. It didn't really matter, of course – not as much as getting Einstein home mattered. Even so, there was a tiny part of her that couldn't help feeling upset.

Imogen tried to tell that part of herself to be quiet. Eleven-year-olds don't get upset about silly, babyish things like birthday parties, she informed it.

But the upset part of her wanted to argue back. Eleven-year-olds should at least be able to *have* birthday parties, it nagged. They shouldn't have to watch their whole class go off and be friends with somebody else.

'Isn't it your birthday too?'

Imogen looked up to see who had spoken to her. It was Gracie.

'Yes,' she said. 'On Sunday.'

'Are you doing anything?'

Imogen considered this. 'I'm going to have a tea party with my penguins,' she said eventually.

After all, Einstein and Isaac might have come home

by then, so she wasn't strictly telling a lie. It was only a lie if you knew for a fact that what you were saying was untrue.

Gracie smiled. 'That sounds really fun. Penguins are my favourite animal.'

Imogen was a little surprised at this. After all, at some point in the last few weeks, Amy had decided that Imogen was *weird* for being friends with a penguin, and she had always assumed that Gracie would agree.

'You can come if you want,' Imogen found herself saying.

'I can?' said Gracie.

Imogen started to nod, but just then the bell rang, and the boys came rushing inside from their football practice. Among them was Arthur, and she hurried over to interrogate him.

Chapter Twelve

Accomplices

Arthur was in two minds about talking to his sister. Of course, he wanted to tell her what he had worked out. But he was still feeling upset. She hadn't even *told* him about the glasses. If Arthur hadn't had to rescue her confiscated notebook, would he ever have found out about them at all?

'Mum wants to know if you'd like to come for a walk,' said Imogen, poking her head round his bedroom door later that afternoon.

Arthur pushed a toy car across the windowsill

and pretended not to hear. It wasn't that he thought he would gain anything by ignoring her – it was just that he didn't know how to say whatever it was that he wanted to say.

'Why are you angry?' Imogen asked. 'I already said thank you for getting the notebook back.'

She was just about to give up and leave the room when Arthur piped up, in a sulky voice. 'When were you going to tell me about the glasses?'

Imogen frowned at him. 'You read my notebook?'

'I had to,' said Arthur. 'You didn't tell me about anything that was in it.'

'That's because I haven't worked it out yet,' Imogen admitted. 'I was going to tell you once I'd worked it out.'

'What if *I* could work it out?' said Arthur. 'But you never ask me because you think I'm stupid!'

'I don't think you're stupid, Arthur,' said Imogen, stepping a little further into the room. 'I just – I like doing things by myself sometimes.'

'Einstein is my friend too.'

'Okay,' said Imogen. 'I'm sorry.'

She sat down on the bed beside him, pulled the glasses out of her pocket and – reluctantly at first, then with more assurance – handed them over.

Arthur took the glasses without looking at her and turned them over in his hands. His heart gave a loud thud. He was right; he was sure of it now. He could picture the woman perfectly in his head and he knew – he *knew* – that the glasses were hers. He turned to Imogen and told her everything.

'That woman,' he finished. 'It must have been her!'

Imogen sat in silence for a few minutes. 'But that can't be right . . .' she whispered. 'I thought it was Bill Hunter who kidnapped them . . .'

Her gut had told her so strongly that Bill Hunter was the criminal, but now Arthur was here, telling her something completely different. The mark on Bill's hand had seemed like such an obvious sign. Arthur had to be wrong. But if he *was* right they might just be a step closer to solving the case – guiltily, she almost felt disappointed.

'A woman in an art gallery,' she repeated. 'It doesn't make sense.'

'The glasses are the same!' Arthur insisted. 'And Bill Hunter was standing right next to us when Einstein was taken. It couldn't have been him.'

'But it has to be.'

'He'd have had to get somebody else to do it for him!' said Arthur.

He spoke as if the idea was a ridiculous one, but Imogen's eyes widened. That was it – she had it!

'He has an accomplice,' she gasped.

Arthur looked blank. 'What's an accomplice?' he asked.

'It's someone who helps somebody else commit a crime. I know that Bill Hunter has seen Einstein more recently than he's letting on. He has a bite on his hand – I *saw* it.' Imogen paused. 'What did you say the woman looked like?'

'She had red hair. And she was quite old – it was a bit grey – and she had these weird glasses . . .'

Imogen closed her eyes, and suddenly everything fell into place. 'The glasses,' she whispered. 'I think I saw them on the front desk in Bill Hunter's studio.'

*

Imogen spent the whole night planning. With all the adrenaline that was rushing through her body, putting off sleep was hardly difficult.

She hadn't been completely sure about things at first, but then she had pulled up pictures of Bill Hunter's studio on Google, and Arthur had found the assistant on the agency website – the same woman he had seen following them round the gallery – and it had only taken one long zoom on her glasses to confirm that they were the same pair Imogen had found on the floor that day. The woman must, she realised, have been the one who served them hot chocolate that first day in Bill Hunter's studio – if only they'd got a better look at her face to start with, everything could have been so much easier.

It had taken three shouts for Mr Stewart to coax Imogen downstairs for supper, and even then she couldn't stop glancing sideways at the stairs. When Mrs Stewart finally got fed up and demanded that she finish her food, Imogen was so distracted that she spilled half her vegetables on to her lap. A big piece of broccoli bounced off the edge of her shoe and hit Gizmo right on his whiskers.

'Are you all right, Imogen?' asked Mr Stewart. 'You seem to have ants in your pants.'

'I'm fine,' said Imogen automatically.

She'd be happy to tell her parents her plan once she had made one, and once she knew for certain where Einstein was – but they had become so obsessed with reporting everything to that useless policeman. She didn't want them interfering and taking over just when things were starting to make sense.

'Are you still worried about that notebook?' asked Mrs Stewart.

Imogen opened her mouth, then paused. Of course, her parents had no idea that Arthur and Theo had stolen the notebook back. 'Yes,' she agreed, happy to have been offered the excuse.

'Well, just one day to go until you get it back. And Bill Hunter called again today. Apparently he's made some more progress.' Mrs Stewart furrowed her brow. 'He couldn't tell me what the progress was, unfortunately, but he sounded very excited . . .'

'And we've got that policeman on the case,' Mr Stewart piped up. 'He's been checking the CCTV footage: it seems he can't see anyone leaving the building at the right time. But there are ways of getting past these things, so I gave him a few more of my theories.'

'That's good,' Imogen smiled.

Mr Stewart looked immediately suspicious, and would have questioned her further had Gizmo not swallowed the offending broccoli in one go, then swiftly vomited it back up all over the carpet.

'I'm very tired,' said Imogen. 'I think I'll go to bed.'

'Not without putting your plate in the dishwasher!' said Mrs Stewart, grabbing Mr Stewart's newspaper and throwing it on top of the pile of sick as a makeshift mop.

'I hadn't finished reading that, Rachel!' said Mr Stewart.

Imogen did as she was told, then darted up the stairs while her parents were still too busy bickering to notice.

Back in the safety of her bedroom, and with Mrs Stewart's laptop open on the floor, Imogen started to look more closely at the pictures of Bill Hunter's studio. What evidence would she find in all that concrete? Would Bill Hunter and his assistant even still be there? She supposed it all depended on why they had wanted to kidnap the penguins in the first place, and what they were planning to do with them. Suddenly Imogen had a vision of them trapped in a crate stacked up on a boat, already miles and miles away from London . . .

She shook the image out of her head. She was getting ahead of herself again. Wherever Einstein and Isaac were, and no matter why they'd been kidnapped, she *needed* to get into that studio. At the very least, it would provide evidence for her investigation.

The question, as always, was how. Imogen sketched the building again and again and considered all the various ways she might sneak in. The front entrance was out of bounds, of course: she couldn't risk compromising the operation by being seen. But the windows were all terribly high up, and the side entrance was much too visible from the road. After a long time tossing and turning and scribbling, a plan – faint at first – started to form.

Eventually Arthur knocked on her door. 'Are you okay?' he asked, his eyes widening at the drawings covering her bedroom floor. 'I can't sleep.'

Imogen looked at her brother. 'I'm sorry for not sharing stuff with you, Arthur,' she said.

Arthur looked surprised. 'That's okay.' He shrugged. Really it seemed like a long time ago now.

'I have to do something tomorrow that would make Mum and Dad very cross if they found out about it,' Imogen went on. 'And I was wondering – would you like to be my accomplice?'

Chapter Thirteen

Operation Einstein

Imogen hailed the taxi as soon as Mrs Stewart was out of sight. She knew that she would get in trouble, and that her teachers would find out all about it and peer down their serious noses at her on Monday morning, but somehow she didn't mind.

In fact, she found the idea sort of funny – because *they* didn't understand that what she was doing was important, or how urgent it was, or the fact that she was on a mission and that she knew, deep down in her stomach, that she was going to get it right. True,

Imogen didn't know exactly how yet, but it was an instinct more than anything. Inspector Bucket, the detective from her favourite books, always used his instinct. Not everyone *had* good instincts, of course, but Imogen did. If there was one thing she was sure of, it was that.

Meanwhile Arthur was so nervous that he kept his eyes screwed shut for several minutes after the school first disappeared from view in the rear window – as if not being able to see would stop anyone from being able to see him, now or ever again.

'It's okay,' Imogen whispered. 'Remember we're rescuing Einstein.'

Arthur nodded and tried to push the nerves back into place again, the same way he had when he'd stolen Imogen's notebook. He wondered what Theo was doing and whether he was going to miss him today, or wonder where he was.

'That's ten pounds, love,' said the driver, once he

had pulled up beside the studio, and after Imogen had hurriedly asked him to park a little further down the road.

'Ten pounds . . .' Imogen repeated.

She had taken all the money from her moneybox and a little from her mother's stash in the cutlery drawer, but she couldn't remember how much it added up to. She started fumbling around with the change and dropped half of it under the driving seat.

'Shouldn't you kids be at school?' asked the driver, while he was waiting.

'No,' said Imogen quickly. 'We're gifted children. Our teachers decided we were too clever for school and didn't need to go any more.'

'Not so gifted you can count change, apparently,' said the driver, though not in an altogether mean way. 'That's eight pounds. I'm sure I'll find the other two on the floor.'

'Thank you!' said Imogen, and he winked at her.

*

Arthur trailed behind his sister, watching her with a mixture of nerves and curiosity. Instead of heading straight for the front entrance, she had turned right and was leading him down a narrow alley, walking sideways with her back pressed up against the wall. Now that he came to think of it, he didn't suppose marching through the front door would have been

a very good idea, but he definitely couldn't see the problem with walking in a straight line. There was nobody around, after all.

Eventually they reached some big green bins beside the building's fire escape.

'In here!' Imogen whispered.

'In the *bin*?' said Arthur. 'Are you crazy?'

'Quick! There's no time!' She put her hands out and gave Arthur a leg-up.

Arthur scrambled over the edge of the bin, his landing cushioned by a cardboard box and some pieces of old blanket. A moment passed and then Imogen crashed down beside him.

'Your school skirt has banana on it,' Arthur pointed out, but Imogen ignored him.

The sky, which had been looking a little cross and grey all morning, suddenly opened up in a prickle of cold raindrops. Imogen picked up a square of cardboard and placed it on top of her head as a sort of umbrella. Then she started the watch.

For what felt like a long time, Imogen stood on tiptoes and peered over the edge of the bin, motionlessly watching the door. Meanwhile Arthur, who was sitting down, watched his sister and wondered something between three and four times whether she might be going mad.

Just when Arthur was starting to wish they had gone to school, after all, Imogen gasped and ducked down. The fire escape clattered open and a big hand tossed another bin bag on top of the pile beside them.

Then, as the footsteps retreated, Imogen jumped up, picked up the bin bag and threw it into the doorway.

The sound of the door slamming shut never came. The bag, Arthur could see as he stood to investigate, had stopped it from closing properly.

'Now we can go!' she said.

'Where?' asked Arthur anxiously.

'I don't know yet,' Imogen admitted. 'But we'll find out when we get there.'

Einstein was bored.

He was used to being in an enclosure, of course, but at least the zoo in Sydney had water to swim in and people to stare at. This room only had the woman, and Einstein wasn't interested in staring at her – only in giving her the odd glare from time to time. And, besides, she hadn't come in for a while. She had stopped appearing so much after Einstein had bitten Bill Hunter's hand, often choosing to check on them by peering round the door instead.

Einstein gave Isaac a tired little honk, and Isaac

looked up and honked back at him, then carried on watching the spider that was busy making its web in the corner beside him. Every so often, Isaac would peck the centre of the web, and the spider – not knowing what had hit it – would spin round in a daze before diligently restarting the process.

Einstein waddled round in a circle and stared at the floor. At the edge of the skirting board was a fishfinger – one he must have missed at suppertime. He picked it up with his beak and carried it over to the woman's chair, then jumped up to place it on the seat before pecking it into a sort of mush.

He jumped down again when he heard voices in the corridor outside, and waddled as fast as he could back to his place in the corner.

But then – was that . . .? It couldn't be. Einstein approached the door again, his head craning forward to listen.

The voice he had heard – just for a moment – had

sounded an awful lot like Imogen's. He shook his head and squawked at Isaac, who had somehow got the spider's web wrapped round his beak and had fallen over in a panic.

Just then the door burst open, and in came the woman. She refilled the water bowl from a bottle and sat down in the chair.

'Hello, penguins,' she said a little gloatingly, though not in quite the same croon she normally used.

Einstein ignored her.

'I won't be seeing you for much longer,' she announced. 'Isn't that sad?'

This caught Einstein's attention. He stared at her in shock. But, before the woman had time to explain herself, there was another noise from the hallway outside.

She frowned and jumped up, mushy fishfinger paste clinging messily to the bottom of her skirt, then marched out of the room.

*

Imogen wandered on through the corridor.

The more she explored, the more she realised how abandoned the place was. She supposed they must be quite near the room where the filming had been taking place on Monday, but she didn't think she could have found her way back to it very easily. It could have been above her, below her, in front of her or on either side.

'Do you know where we are?' whispered Arthur.

'Of course I do,' she lied and picked up the pace a little.

Apart from their footsteps, it was eerily quiet, and Imogen shivered in the silence. Of course, it wouldn't make sense for any of the people she had seen last time to be coming into work, would it? Now that Einstein and Isaac were gone, they'd probably run out of filming to do. But, then again, *someone* had been putting the bins out. Imogen glanced over her shoulder nervously.

Suddenly she found herself wondering whether

anyone had started looking for replacement penguin actors yet, and the idea made her so cross that she pushed open the nearest door and marched through it.

Arthur followed her obediently. It led to a short corridor at the end of which was another smaller door marked Equipment.

'Are you *sure* you know where we are?' asked Arthur.

In the distance they heard the sound of lift doors pinging opening.

'Quick! In here,' said Imogen, hurrying down the corridor towards the door. With everything that was rushing through her imagination, she had become jumpy. Too jumpy, perhaps.

The strip lights on the ceiling flickered on as they moved inside, and Arthur pushed the door firmly shut behind them. Then he turned round. The room they had found themselves in seemed to be a storage space for cameras – some big, some small, some still in their boxes.

Imogen took a further step into the room and ran her finger through a pile of dust that was gathering on the window ledge.

'Imogen,' whispered Arthur, 'isn't that the camera the man was using on Monday?'

Imogen looked at her brother. He was pointing to the largest camera, the one in the corner. It was sitting on a desk, already connected to a computer by a cable.

'I don't know,' said Imogen. 'They all look the same.'

'No, they don't. I remember it.' Arthur felt quite certain, and he went to switch the computer on.

'What are you doing?' asked Imogen.

'I'm seeing if there's any evidence stored on the camera,' said Arthur. He peered at her in confusion. 'Isn't that why you wanted to come in here?'

'Oh, yeah,' said Imogen, going a little pink. 'Obviously.'

She followed her brother over to the desk and

leaned over his shoulder.

Someone had already started loading the videos on to the computer, and they appeared on the screen in a file. Arthur clicked on the first one.

'Action!' a voice called, and Einstein waddled on-screen in front of a green background. A few seconds later, Isaac followed him, at which point Einstein stopped unexpectedly and Isaac crashed into his flipper, then tripped over. 'Stop, *stop*!' the voice called.

Imogen and Arthur giggled. It was sad, in a way, being able to see Einstein so clearly and yet not knowing where in the world he was. But somehow laughing felt like the only solution.

'Click the next one! Click the next one!' said Imogen.

They moved from one clip to the next, watching Einstein and Isaac fight over a fishfinger, hearing a piece of lighting equipment fall over and send Isaac into a fit of nervous squawks, watching Einstein's smug feather-ruffle when they finally got the scene right.

'What's that clip down there?' asked Imogen, pointing to the very last one.

Arthur clicked on it, but nothing played. There was only darkness, and a strange muttering noise in the background. But, just as they were about to move on, a bright light illuminated the shadowy room on the screen, and someone seemed to flicker across it.

Imogen and Arthur huddled closer to the computer and replayed it slowly. This time, when the light appeared, Arthur paused and zoomed in.

'That's her!' Imogen gasped.

A woman with a gingery-grey mane of hair could be seen rushing towards the door at the back of the room – the same one Imogen had charged out of on the day of the kidnapping – and she was holding a small, shadowy, penguin-shaped figure under each arm.

'I knew it!' said Arthur.

Imogen stared at the screen, and a hot sort of anger built up in her chest and in her stomach. She could remember the moment exactly: how the cameraman had tried to help by using his flash as a torch, and how Bill Hunter had told him not to. She clenched her fists and teeth. She wished that the woman was in the room with them now, so that she could tell her what she thought of her.

‘We have to find her!’ said Imogen.

‘Wait,’ said Arthur. Imogen was always rushing into things, and he couldn’t always get his head round it. ‘What will you say to her?’

‘That we know what she did, and that we’re going to get Einstein and Isaac back!’

‘But we don’t even know where they are,’ Arthur pointed out.

Imogen paused. Arthur had a point. Knowing who did the kidnapping wasn’t the same as knowing where Einstein and Isaac *were,* and accusing the woman wouldn’t necessarily bring them back. Imogen had learned from her detective books that sometimes it was better not to reveal everything you knew straight away.

Imogen recalled with surprise that she didn’t even know the woman’s name, or anything about her. Why would she want to kidnap the penguins on Bill Hunter’s behalf? *Was* she doing it on his behalf, or was *he* helping *her*? And, of course, Bill Hunter had been talking as if he was planning on rescuing them. The motive simply didn't make any sense.

'Perhaps we should see if there's any more footage?' Arthur piped up. Imogen was doing the thinking face that made him nervous.

'CCTV footage,' Imogen whispered suddenly.

Her mind whirred back to the dinner table the evening before: Mr Stewart had mentioned CCTV footage, and Imogen had been too distracted to listen to him properly. What was it he had said? The policeman hadn't been able to spot anyone leaving the building on the CCTV footage . . .

'Oh, Arthur,' she said, 'what if they never left the building?'

Chapter Fourteen

Caught Red-handed

Mr Stewart put the phone down. 'Erm, Rachel . . .?' he began.

'What?' said Mrs Stewart impatiently. She was frowning at the table as she hurriedly packed her things into a bag. 'Where did I put the car keys?'

'Where are the children?' Mr Stewart asked.

Mrs Stewart stopped moving for a moment and looked thoughtful. 'Perhaps they're in my other handbag.'

'The children, not the car keys.'

'They're at school,' said Mrs Stewart. 'It's Friday.

Just because *you* don't work on Fridays—'

'Ah,' Mr Stewart interrupted. 'But the thing is the headmistress just phoned to tell me that they're *not* at school.'

'Exactly. I dropped them off this morning. I—' Mrs Stewart paused. 'Hang on – did you say "not"?'

'Yes,' said Mr Stewart. 'As in no. As in yes, I said that they weren't there.'

'Stop speaking gibberish!' Mrs Stewart's face went white. '*How* are they not there?!'

'Well, I was going to ask you the same thing,' explained Mr Stewart. 'Seeing as you were the one who dropped them off.'

'Yes!' she cried. 'And I did! But what did the headmistress actually *say*? Are they looking for them? Are you sure it's both of them?' Then she stopped, and some of the colour came back into her cheeks. 'Oh, that *girl*!' she growled, and hurried up the stairs to Imogen's bedroom.

*

Imogen ran and ran and ran down the corridor. She was looking for Bill Hunter's office, but of course last time they had come in through a different entrance, so now everything looked back to front and confusing. Every time she passed a door, she would push at it or peer through it – hoping, hoping, hoping that one of them would open, and Einstein would be there, waiting for her.

But if he wasn't, if she couldn't find him . . . well, then she would find Bill Hunter and his accomplice – whatever she was called – and she would *make* them tell her where he was. Now that she suspected Einstein and Isaac had never really left the building, she felt braver, like nobody could fool her any more.

Suddenly she recognised the door she was looking for.

'In here!' she hissed at Arthur, who was panting as he caught up with her.

Bill Hunter's office looked much the same as it had before, but this time it was empty. It was still oddly cold, the fan whirring overhead even though spring had scarcely begun, and decorated here and there with potted houseplants. Imogen walked up to one of them and touched it. The leaves, she found, were made of hard, shiny plastic, and didn't smell of anything.

'Nobody's here,' said Arthur disappointedly. 'We'll have to try another room.'

Imogen almost agreed with him. In her imagination Bill Hunter had been sitting at his desk with Einstein and Isaac in the corner beside him, but instead the place was deserted. Then something caught her eye.

'Hang on,' Imogen whispered. She moved closer to the wall.

There had been notes and pieces of paper on the wall last time too, but Imogen hadn't really looked at them or read them, and this time there were more. Many more.

She reached out and pulled a newspaper cutting down from its place on the pinboard:

BRITISH CHILDREN
RETURN MISSING
PENGUIN TO SYDNEY

'That's us,' said Imogen incredulously.

Then she pulled down the next one:

Imogen Stewart:
The Girl Who Solved
The Penguin Mystery

Arthur rushed over to join her and stood on his tiptoes so that he could read too.

Imogen let her eyes scan the rest of the wall. Not every article was about her, but they were all about investigations, all detective stories. And right in the middle was a piece of newspaper that had quite clearly been torn up and then stuck back together with Sellotape:

BILL HUNTER FIRED FROM TOP DETECTIVE AGENCY

Arthur followed the direction of his sister's gaze.

'But he said he left,' said Arthur. 'He didn't say that he was fired.'

'He lied,' Imogen breathed.

Detective Bill Hunter has left his job in disgrace after failing to get to the bottom of a mystery that was instead solved by a nine-year-old girl from London. According to his boss, this was the final straw in a long history of incompetence. The position is now open for applications.

'He said he wasn't even interested in being a detective any more . . .' said Arthur.

Imogen's mind felt both blank and sharply focused,

the way it did before a big realisation, and her head almost ached with concentration. She strode over to the desk and started rifling through the drawers.

Inside she found pictures of Einstein and Isaac from over a year ago, along with the original newspaper article announcing Einstein's escape from Sydney Zoo. When Imogen looked at it, she almost started to smile, but there was no time for that. She pushed it to one side and underneath it discovered a stack of Bill Hunter's notes from when he had been tracking Einstein between London and Edinburgh.

In fairness he had worked a lot of it out. He really might have solved the mystery if it hadn't been for Imogen and Arthur getting in his way at the last moment. Imogen remembered with a shiver how angry he had been, and it made his strange shift to kindness a few weeks ago seem all the more peculiar.

'Is there anything in there about the advert he's making with Isaac and Einstein?' asked Arthur.

'No,' said Imogen. 'There isn't even anything about his job.'

Nothing. Imogen frowned. *Nothing.* In his own office. It was almost as if, she thought – in fact, it was *very much* as if – Bill Hunter had never put any effort into planning the advert at all.

'There was no point in him thinking about it,' she said. 'He knew it wasn't going ahead.'

They stood in silence for a moment as this sank in.

'But what does he want with Einstein this time?' said Arthur eventually. 'It's not like he's a detective any more.'

'No,' said Imogen. 'But he wishes he was.'

Arthur still looked confused, but explaining her half-finished thoughts to her brother was helping everything become clearer in Imogen's head.

'So he created a crime he knew he could solve,' she went on, realising the truth of the words only as they came out of her mouth. His reputation had been damaged, he was trying to undo what had gone before

– and his strange claims about finding Einstein and Isaac by the weekend suddenly made perfect sense . . .

'You know, even if we hadn't gone after Bill to apologise, I think he'd have found us eventually.'

'That's right, Imogen,' came a cold, clear voice.

Imogen's heart skipped a beat. She looked up.

In all her concentration she hadn't heard the door open, but there was Bill Hunter – smiling with the red-headed woman just behind him, peering eagerly over his shoulder like a child at the cinema.

'And I can still solve it. And you're not going to get in my way.'

This time Einstein was sure of it. He had heard Imogen, he had heard her running feet, and he had heard Arthur's quieter footsteps trying to keep up with his sister.

He squawked and ran towards the door, hopping up on to the woman's chair and then leaping at the door handle – but it was no use. As always, she had locked it as she left.

Einstein's eyes widened. That was right, she had left. And, if Imogen and Arthur were out in the corridor too, what was to stop them from bumping into one another?

He squawked again, more frantically this time, and jumped back down off the chair. His head ticked from one side to the other as he scanned the room, and his neck craned forward in concentration. Giving a short sigh, he looked up at the distant window.

But then something caught Einstein's attention: a small piece of metal, firmly attached to the wall, was poking out from behind the filing cabinet. Einstein approached it with interest and pecked at it, then squawked at Isaac to join him.

Isaac looked up and swallowed guiltily, the spider's web now empty and balled-up on the floor beside him. He waddled over.

Einstein started to push the cabinet as hard as he could. After several shoves, Isaac got the message and followed his lead, but Isaac was bigger, and it moved more under his weight than Einstein's, causing the cabinet to spin to one side, but go nowhere. Einstein gave a frustrated honk and nudged Isaac into the middle, then started to push against *him* instead. Isaac wheezed, and Einstein pushed, and he pushed and he pushed and he pushed, and after a second or two the

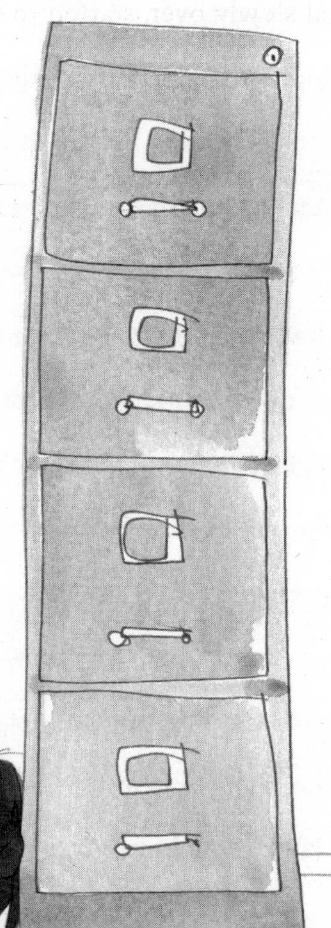

cabinet started to inch slowly sideways under their joint weight. Bit by bit, they nudged it out of the way, and the piece of metal revealed itself.

Einstein squawked loudly, making Isaac jump, and with a screech of metal against metal the cabinet leaned slowly over, started to topple and then fell to the floor with a creak and a deafening crash.

Both penguins landed on their backs in the cloud of dust that the cabinet sent shooting up from the floor. Isaac rolled over and coughed, and something small and spider-shaped fell out of his mouth and limped half-heartedly towards the skirting board.

But Einstein wasn't watching that. Einstein was looking at something far, far more important.

An air vent.

'Imogen, Arthur, I'd like you to meet my assistant, Vanessa,' said Bill Hunter. 'Vanessa has been looking after your penguin friends.'

'Now, Bill, do you really have to call me—' Vanessa began, but he shot her a cross look, and she quickly fell silent.

Imogen and Arthur stared at him.

'This is the part when you say *thank you, Vanessa.*'

'Thank you for what?' Imogen growled. 'For kidnapping two innocent animals in order to reboot your career?'

'Well, now, it wasn't strictly Vanessa who did that.'

'No, but she helped!'

Imogen glared at him. She hated how Bill Hunter seemed to actually be having *fun*. The way he walked so bouncily on the balls of his feet, the fact that he didn't even care about being caught out – it made her skin crawl.

'Yes, Imogen, you're very clever,' said Bill Hunter. 'You'll almost certainly do very well in your exams this year. But here's the thing.'

He sat down in his desk chair and swivelled round

in a big circle, then used his feet to shuffle it back into position when he ended up pointing the wrong way.

'You may think that you've uncovered my plan—'

'I *have* uncovered your plan,' Imogen interrupted.

'—but *I* still have your penguins. And, unless you agree to my terms, I'm not going to give them back.' He rested his hands on his stomach and smiled. 'Not even as part of my big reveal. In fact, they might just . . . *disappear*.'

'You're an awful person,' Arthur spat out, and Bill Hunter looked at him in mock surprise.

'Ah, the little brother speaks!'

'And you,' Arthur blurted, turning to Vanessa. 'How could you help him? In the art gallery you seemed so . . . so nice,' he finished weakly.

Vanessa sneered at him and rolled her eyes.

'She *is* nice, Arthur,' said Bill Hunter. 'We don't all live in your silly little world of goodies and baddies. People are complicated.'

Arthur scowled at this patronising speech. Of course people were complicated. Imogen was one of the best people he knew, but was still always grumpy when she was tired, and Grandpa Stewart always overcooked the beef, but made excellent apple crumble. But you couldn't be complicated by being both a nice person and a penguin kidnapper. It didn't make any sense.

'Well then,' said Imogen, breaking the silence, 'what *are* your terms?'

'See, your sister knows how to do things politely.' Bill Hunter smiled. 'My terms are very simple. I tell the world that I have rescued the penguins, I give them back and, when asked, you confirm my story.'

'And how do we fit into your made-up story?'

Bill Hunter considered this. 'You can tell them that I rescued you too. That you tried to save the penguins yourselves, but were overcome by the evil kidnapper, and *I* rescued all four of you. And then that I brought you here, patched you up and called the police, saving the day.'

'But that isn't *true*,' said Arthur.

'Oh, Arthur, you're far too young to understand that it doesn't really matter what's true. You get your penguins back, and I get my career back. My old detective firm rehires me, and you get to roll around on the floor, eating fishfingers with a flightless seabird for as long as your heart desires. Everybody's happy. Now that's a far better truth, is it not?'

Imogen looked at Bill Hunter, at his slimy smile and his cross eyebrows and his wiry hair, and found it astonishing that just a couple of weeks ago she had actually felt *sorry* for him.

She imagined having to watch him lie his way to success and not being able to do anything about it, being forced to see him prance about and pose for the press and imply that she was little and helpless and stupid, and the very idea of it made her sick to her stomach.

But then she imagined the alternative, an alternative in which she might never see Einstein or Isaac again or know whether they were all right, and she knew that she didn't really have a choice at all.

'All right,' said Imogen. 'We'll stick to your story. Just . . . let them go.'

'Imogen?' Arthur whispered, incredulous.

'That's right,' said Bill Hunter. 'Listen to your sister, Arthur. She's not as stupid as she looks. Vanessa, pass me my phone.'

Vanessa reached into her pocket and handed it over.

'Now, before I call the police and tell them our story, you both need to make a promise.'

Imogen's stomach squirmed. She already knew that she had lost, but somehow having to make a promise out of it made it so much worse.

'Do you promise,' said Bill Hunter, 'that this time I am not going to be stopped by a nine-year-old?'

Arthur glanced at his sister. She was wearing her thoughtful expression, the one where she frowned and bit her lip, and just for a moment it made Arthur feel hopeful, like she might have discovered something that was going to save the day. But then she just nodded and, with an aching hole in his chest, Arthur nodded too.

Chapter Fifteen

Einstein Intervenes

With a loud crack, the air-vent cover popped open, and Einstein peered around the room ahead of him.

He gave a low squawk of disappointment. Another empty room – or at least it was empty *now*. His small eyes narrowed as he spotted that the lights were on and the door was open, as if someone had only recently left it, and he stared down at the camera equipment with a look of vague recognition.

Then Einstein almost fell out of the air vent in excitement.

At the edge of one of the tables was a small orange hair tie, just like the kind that Imogen always wore. He hopped down and carefully picked it up with his beak, then chirruped happily up at Isaac to tell him what he had found.

Isaac squawked back – an impatient sort of squawk that suggested moving on – and Einstein honked in agreement and got ready to jump back inside the air vent. But first he paused and looked thoughtful. Then he picked up one of the smallest cameras, carrying it with him.

Imogen and Arthur waited in Bill Hunter's office for what felt like an eternity, though in reality it might only have been a few minutes. The cold drizzle outside had not let up, and Imogen watched it solemnly through the window, listening to the low patter of raindrops on the roof and the sound of cars cascading through puddles on the road outside.

'Do you really think he'll get away with it?' asked Arthur.

Imogen looked at her brother and didn't quite know what to say. She hadn't given up yet, not exactly – she was merely prioritising. And, while the cogs of her brain were still busy whirring away, she didn't want to get his hopes up and then let them down again.

'I really think we'll get Einstein back,' she told him, instead of answering his question.

'You made Bill Hunter a promise,' said Arthur sadly.

'Yes,' said Imogen. 'But remember I'm not actually ni—'

Before she could finish her sentence there was a loud crash from the wall above their heads.

'Einstein!' cried Arthur.

A small feathery head was sticking out of the air vent, the cover of which had fallen and bounced across the room after hitting one of Bill Hunter's plastic plant leaves.

Arthur could hardly believe his eyes, and he stuck out his arms for Einstein to jump into. When he caught him, he hugged him tightly. Einstein's feathers smelled of dust and very faintly of fishfingers, but of a soft sort of cosiness at the same time.

Imogen clambered up on to a chair to help Isaac down – he had become stuck on his way out, the gap not quite wide enough for his stomach – and she tugged him out by his flippers.

'Are you all right?' she asked, and Isaac squawked

grumpily and coughed out a cloud of dust.

But Arthur had hardly noticed the commotion. 'What's that you've got?' he was busy asking Einstein, as he tried to remove something from his beak.

Einstein made a brief show of not wanting to hand it over, but eventually did as he was asked.

'It's a camera,' said Arthur.

Imogen stepped closer to see. 'Why do you think he brought that?' she asked.

Arthur shrugged and turned it over in his hands. 'Perhaps he thought it would be useful.'

'Or maybe it just looked shiny.'

Einstein appeared offended at Imogen's suggestion and shot her a dirty look.

'All right, you're very clever. I'm sorry,' said Imogen, patting him on his feathery head.

Just then a siren sounded from the road outside, and Imogen hurried back to the window, clambering up on to a chair to get a better look. A police car had appeared outside the entrance of the building and a policeman was clambering out of it. He stumbled on to the pavement, said something into his walkie-talkie and then looked expectantly at the door.

'What is it?' asked Arthur.

'It's that policeman,' said Imogen. 'The same one as last time.'

'Is he coming inside?'

'I don't think so— Oh, no!' Imogen inhaled sharply. 'It's Mum and Dad.'

Mr Stewart's car pulled up beside the policeman's, and Mrs Stewart came hurrying out of it to talk to him. She seemed to be asking the policeman a question – Imogen *wished* she could hear what they were saying to each other – and then held her hands to her mouth in shock at the response. She looked nervously at the door to the building.

'Do you think we'll be in trouble?' asked Arthur.

For a second, Imogen had worried the same thing,

but now that Einstein and Isaac were here she wasn't sure she cared: if only Mr and Mrs Stewart could see her, she supposed they might have been able to help. But of course the door was locked, and the window was closed, and nobody could hear her.

'Up here!' cried Imogen, fruitlessly banging her fist against the glass. 'Look at me!'

She spun round as she heard the door open. Bill Hunter and Vanessa barged in.

'Get down from there!' Bill Hunter growled.

Imogen jumped at the anger in his face and voice, but it quickly receded as he regained control of himself, remaining only in his eyes.

'Breaking your promise so soon?' he asked.

Imogen caught Arthur's eye across the room, and he could tell from her glance that she was thinking the same thing he was.

'I didn't break my promise,' said Imogen. 'We didn't move. Einstein and Isaac came to us.'

Arthur felt frozen to the floor, his hands stuck firmly to his sides. Vanessa was watching him – how could he get her to stop watching him?

'How on earth could they have come to you?' said Bill Hunter.

'Through the air vent. Maybe your assistant should have tightened it.'

Vanessa whipped round in annoyance, and, with both adults facing his sister, Arthur slipped his hand inside his pocket, pulled Einstein's camera out ever so slightly and quietly pressed RECORD.

'I'm sorry, Bill, it wasn't me. I—'

He held his hand up to silence her and looked up at the coverless air vent. 'Fine, fine,' he said.

Imogen could tell he was pretending to be calmer than he was.

'Are you going to keep your promise then?'

Arthur gave Imogen an almost imperceptible thumbs up.

'What promise?' she asked.

'Don't play games with me!'

'Now that we have Einstein and Isaac, I don't see why I need to keep my promise,' Imogen went on.

'Oh, really?' said Bill Hunter. 'Well, I've already told my story over the phone. And who do you think the police will believe? A licensed detective or two silly children who are *meant* to be at school?'

'You're not a licensed detective,' Imogen pointed out. 'You just used to be!'

'But I will be again, very shortly. The lengths I've gone to to prove my ability.'

'Lengths like kidnapping?' asked Imogen.

'Yes. Lengths like that.'

They had him now. Imogen clenched her fist in place of punching the air.

'Fine,' she said, giving her best imitation of a sad shrug and a sigh. 'If you keep your side of the deal, I'll keep mine.'

*

Mrs Stewart gave a small squeak of relief when Imogen and Arthur walked out of the building. Bill Hunter kept one hand on each of their shoulders, and Vanessa walked carefully beside them, a penguin tucked under each arm.

After that, everything happened in a hurry.

'The policeman told me what you did,' Mrs Stewart was saying to Bill Hunter, her eyes a little teary. 'Thank you.'

Even Mr Stewart took a step forward to shake him by the hand, and then Mr and Mrs Stewart scooped Imogen and Arthur into a hug.

Imogen swallowed the nervous lump in her throat as she saw that a second police car had arrived, along with a news crew.

'Did the kidnapper hurt you?' Mrs Stewart asked. 'Where did you follow him to? Why didn't you tell us where you'd gone?'

'I think I should ask the questions, madam,' said the policeman, and his colleague nodded seriously. 'If you don't mind.'

'No need.' Bill Hunter stepped in breezily. 'I've been tracking the kidnapper for days. The kids getting involved threw a spanner in the works, but I managed to rescue them too. And here we all are. Right as rain.'

'Yes, you mentioned that earlier,' said the policeman. 'But I still want to talk to the children.'

'Oh – well, of course they'll confirm it all for you.' Bill Hunter patted Arthur's shoulder like he was praising a particularly useless dog.

'No, we won't!' said Imogen suddenly.

For a nervous moment, she had doubted her ability to say anything at all, but then it all came pouring out like vomit.

Everyone turned to her in shock. Even the news reporter, who was just unpacking his microphone, stopped to stare at her.

'This man is a liar,' said Arthur. He felt Bill Hunter's nails dig into his shoulder and shrugged his hand away.

'He kidnapped the penguins himself in order to rescue them and get you all to believe that he's a good detective!' said Imogen. 'But he isn't! And that woman helped him!'

Vanessa looked startled and let go of Einstein and

Isaac, who hurried over to Mr and Mrs Stewart as fast as their webbed feet would carry them.

'They're lying!' she cried. 'My Bill would never—'

'Be *quiet,* Mother!' Bill Hunter snapped, and then blushed in the ensuing silence.

'So this woman is your mother then?' the policeman asked, scribbling something down in his notepad.

'*No*—' Bill started to protest.

'Yes, I am,' Vanessa said breezily. 'And the cats he uses in his adverts all belong to *me*—'

'Of course, Imogen Stewart would tell a story like that,' said Bill Hunter, quickly changing the subject. 'She's upset that she didn't solve the mystery and is telling lies. I expected better, but it's frankly typical.'

The policeman chewed his lip and frowned. 'All right. So who *was* the kidnapper then?'

Bill Hunter made a face as if the question was hardly relevant. 'Well, he escaped, didn't he?'

'But if you've been tracking him for days then you

must have some idea of who he is, some sort of hunch? What did he look like?'

'If it wasn't Bill Hunter who did it, then why did we find Einstein and Isaac in his studio?' Imogen pointed out. 'Who else would have hidden them there?'

Bill Hunter rolled his eyes. 'As I've already explained twice, I brought the children and the penguins *back* here after I rescued them. And they ought to be grateful.'

'But the drawings in Imogen's bedroom . . .' said Mrs Stewart slowly. 'They were of *this* building. This is where they were heading when they skipped school. Where are you claiming you rescued them from?'

Just then Arthur pulled the camera out of his pocket, turned the volume up and pressed PLAY. The voice was muffled, and the video that went along with it was a little blurry, but in the silence that fell everyone could hear what it said:

'And who do you think the police will believe? A licensed detective or two silly children who are meant to be at school?'

'Bill Hunter, I am arresting you on suspicion of animal theft and fraud,' said the policeman, pulling a pair of handcuffs out of his pocket. 'And I am arresting your mother on suspicion of aiding and abetting a crime.'

Imogen looked up at the policeman and smiled. Perhaps she had underestimated him.

Bill Hunter glared at her as he was led over to the police car, and Imogen took a step closer as he was pushed into the back seat.

'You may look innocent,' he said to her, 'but you're a liar too: you broke a promise.'

'But I'm not a nine-year-old!' she hissed over the sound of the slamming door. 'I am *nearly eleven*!'

Chapter Sixteen

Imogen's Birthday

When Imogen woke up on Sunday morning, she was so tired that it took her a whole minute to remember what day it was. In the end it was the small present sitting by the open door of her bedroom that gave it away: her birthday!

She sat up in bed and rubbed her now eleven-year-old eyes, and stretched her now eleven-year-old arms.

Eleven, she thought to herself, turning the number over in her head several times. Yes. It fitted perfectly.

'Arthur! Einstein! Isaac!' shouted Imogen, bounding

over to the present. 'It's my birthday!'

Arthur's footsteps came creaking across the landing followed by the low patter of penguin feet.

'What did you get?' asked Arthur, as Imogen cuddled Einstein good morning.

'I don't know,' she said. 'I haven't opened it yet.'

Einstein gave a helpful little squawk and pulled at the ribbon with his beak. It fell neatly to the floor, and then Imogen ripped the remaining paper off with both hands, balling it up in fistfuls, which Isaac gathered together and absent-mindedly started to chew.

Inside were several new books, a notebook and a pair of night-vision binoculars.

'You don't still think detectives are babyish, do you?' asked Mrs Stewart, appearing from out of her bedroom.

Imogen looked sheepishly up at her mother, who had spent most of yesterday doing a very convincing job of pretending to be cross, but relaxed when she saw that she was smiling.

'No,' said Imogen.

'Well, perhaps *some* detectives are,' said Mr Stewart, who had joined the others, and the whole family exchanged brief, significant glances.

Of course, no one had heard anything more from Bill Hunter since Friday, but the policeman had called in yesterday to collect the camera from Arthur and the glasses from Imogen, and to explain that the evidence was stacked against him and that, thanks to the children, no one with any sense at all was going to believe his story.

'Happy birthday, Imogen,' said Mrs Stewart, and Mr Stewart led everyone downstairs to make pancakes.

'Oh – thank you for my presents,' said Imogen suddenly, remembering her manners as she tucked into her breakfast.

Mr and Mrs Stewart exchanged another glance. 'You haven't had your main present yet,' said Mr Stewart slyly.

'Really?' said Imogen, through a mouthful of pancake. 'What else is there?'

Mr Stewart pretended not to hear her question. 'Well, what are our plans for the rest of the day then?'

With a sudden sinking feeling in her stomach, Imogen remembered that today was Amy's birthday too, and that all her friends would be going to Amy's house. It almost hadn't mattered before, but now that her biggest problem was over, and Einstein was back, she could feel the tiny little nagging, everyday problems creeping back into the worry-space that had been left behind.

'Any friends coming over?' her dad asked, half to Imogen and half to Mrs Stewart, and Mrs Stewart replied with an almost imperceptible shake of the head that Imogen knew she hadn't been supposed to see.

'We've got a very exciting guest list of Einstein and Isaac,' said Mrs Stewart cheerily. 'And Theo's coming over, isn't he, Arthur?'

Imogen forced herself to smile, and it made her feel better. After all, her mother was right. What guest list was better than Einstein and Isaac? Only Gizmo seemed to disagree: he was sitting on top of the tumble dryer, yowling tormentedly, but stopped as soon as Imogen fed him half a pancake.

Mrs Stewart even experimented with making fish pancakes for the penguins, which made the kitchen smell, and everyone had to run around opening the windows.

After that, they went for a long walk and watched one of Imogen's favourite films – and then, at around teatime, there was a loud ringing on the doorbell.

'Ah, that'll be Theo,' said Mrs Stewart, getting up to answer the door.

It was Theo, but there was someone else too. As Theo's mother waved enthusiastically and pulled away in her car, Gracie appeared from round the corner.

'Oh – you came!' said Imogen, who was standing on the doorstep in her socks.

Gracie looked embarrassed. 'Wasn't I supposed to? I thought you invited me . . .'

'Oh, yes, I did! I didn't mean it like that.'

'My mum tried calling on Friday afternoon, but nobody picked up. You must have been busy.'

Imogen smiled. 'Yeah, we were a bit busy, actually. Would you like to come and meet my penguins?'

Gracie nodded her head vigorously and followed Imogen inside the house.

'They can be a little messy sometimes . . .' said Imogen cautiously, but Gracie didn't seem to mind.

Even when Einstein stole a huge bite out of Gracie's slice of cake and the whole family cringed in embarrassment, Gracie found it funny more than anything, and exacted her revenge by wiping a dollop of icing on to Einstein's forehead. That was when Imogen knew they were going to be friends.

'So, this other present,' Mrs Stewart ventured. She had given up trying to tidy up the mess as it created itself. 'It's really for you *and* Arthur.'

'For me?' said Arthur, in surprise.

'And for Einstein and Isaac too,' Mr Stewart added.

Imogen stopped licking the chocolate off her fingers and listened.

'You probably already know that we can't have Einstein and Isaac come to live with us,' said Mr Stewart.

Imogen nodded reluctantly. Of course, now that Bill Hunter had been arrested, no one was going to want to finish filming the advert. That meant the penguins weren't technically needed any more and would be sent back home. It was just a matter of when.

'But we've spoken to Sydney Zoo—'

'And Edinburgh,' Mrs Stewart added.

'Yes, and Edinburgh. And we explained all about what you did, and what good friends you've all become, and they've agreed to let Einstein and Isaac be permanently reunited in the same zoo.'

Arthur's eyes widened.

'But not just any zoo,' said Mrs Stewart, who could scarcely hold back her smile. 'In London Zoo.'

'So we can visit them whenever we like?!' asked Arthur.

'Yes. So you can visit them whenever you like.'

Imogen hardly knew what to say. She had almost choked on her hot chocolate. Even Einstein, who had been listening himself, was looking uncharacteristically lost for squawks.

'Did you hear that?' Arthur asked Isaac, who had just noticed that the cat existed and was staring at it in confusion.

'Isaac,' said Arthur, 'you and Einstein are *moving to London Zoo. Together.*'

'Perhaps Einstein will explain it to him later,' said Mrs Stewart, frowning at Isaac with gentle concern.

'Thank you,' said Imogen. 'This is the best birthday ever.'

When Arthur went back to school on Monday, his backpack was still empty apart from his pencil case. But this time he didn't mind.

Spring was approaching, rearing its head from somewhere beneath the cold tarmac and the puddles on the pavements, and the sky was blue and full of fluffy clouds. It occurred to Arthur that he had never really *looked* at a blue sky before, not properly, and that if he stuck his finger out far enough he might be able to scoop up a great big lump of the colour from it, like paint.

'Can we visit Einstein after school?' asked Theo, catching up with Arthur on their way to assembly.

Arthur nodded and grinned. 'If we get your mum to drive us, we'll make it to the zoo before it closes.'

*

A few rows behind them in the school hall sat Imogen, with Gracie beside her.

Amy was two seats over. As the assembly went on, she turned to glance at Imogen crossly from time to time, but Imogen didn't care.

In fact, she hardly noticed.

She rolled up the sleeves of her jumper to welcome in the semi-warmth that was drifting in gusts through the open door, and felt her detective notebook, warm and heavy in her pocket, waiting patiently for the next mystery to appear.

Epilogue

Somewhere on the far side of London, a cell door opened.

'Right,' said the detective, stepping inside. He placed a clear bag down on the table.

Bill Hunter looked up from where he was sitting and narrowed his eyes at the camera and the pair of glasses inside it.

'So, Mr Hunter, what can you tell me about a penguin called Einstein?'

Bill Hunter shrugged. 'Never heard of him in my life.'

The detective slapped a photograph of Bill and Einstein down on to the table in front of him. 'Never?' he asked.

Bill Hunter looked at the photo in silence for a while.

'I was set up,' he said glumly, because he had been in a way: he'd never have done any of this unless he had to.

'Really? Who by?'

'That Imogen girl.'

The detective raised an eyebrow. 'So you're saying Imogen Stewart kidnapped the penguins?'

Bill Hunter opened his mouth, then closed it, then opened it again. 'We're the same!' he declared suddenly. 'I'm a detective too, you know. I never *wanted* any of this.'

'We may be the same,' the detective said, looking down his nose at him, 'but only one of us is going to prison.'

Discover Einstein's adventures in book one . . .

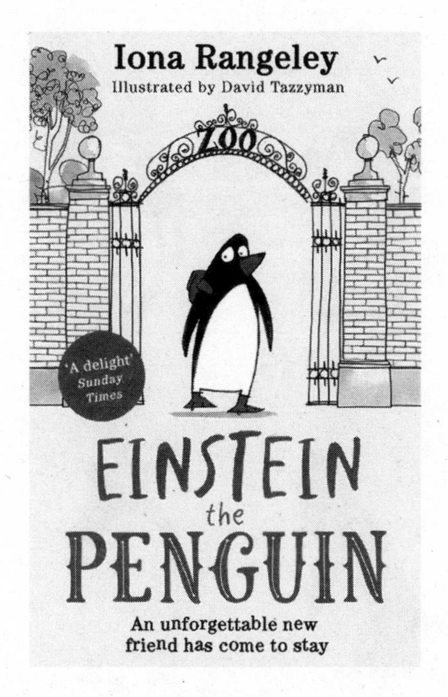